TOO MUCH
of a GOOD
THING
AIN'T BAD

BOOK SALE

JUN 2009

RD

TOO MUCH
of a GOOD
THING
AIN'T BAD

· a novel ·

CLARENCE NERO

BROADWAY BOOKS

New York

Copyright © 2009 by Clarence Nero

Published in the United States by Broadway Books, an imprint of the Crown Publishing Group, a division of Random House, Inc., New York.
www.broadwaybooks.com

BROADWAY BOOKS and its logo, a letter B bisected on the diagonal, are trademarks of Random House, Inc.

Book design by Ellen Cipriano

Library of Congress Cataloging-in-Publication Data
Nero, Clarence, 1970–
Too much of a good thing ain't bad / by Clarence Nero.–1st ed.
p. cm.
1. African American gay men–Fiction.   2. Triangles (Interpersonal relations)–Fiction.   3. Man-woman relationships–Fiction.
4. African Americans–Fiction.   5. Washington (D.C.)–Fiction.
6. Domestic fiction.   I. title.
PS3564.E66T66 2009
813'.54–dc22   2009000403

ISBN 978-0-7679-2972-1

PRINTED IN THE UNITED STATES OF AMERICA

1   3   5   7   9   10   8   6   4   2

First Edition

This book is dedicated to five brothers who—each in his own way, at some point in time—have been an inspiration, a source of strength and support to me in the spirit of brotherhood and friendship.

HILTON WEBB

DELVIN WEBB

KAMAL DORSEY

KENT NICHOLS

FRED HARRISON
October 11, 1967–June 25, 2002

Acknowledgments

I have to give thanks to God for bringing me through and for always making a way for me. Getting this book done was not easy at times, and I leaned on You during the tough times and You were there for me.

I thank my entire family and all my wonderful friends for supporting me, especially Toya, Delvin, and Sharika for going out on the road with me and helping to promote *Three Sides*. And my brother, Hilton, I thank you for the prayers and encouragement during the good and bad times. It really meant a lot to me to have your support in that way. I couldn't have done it without all of you.

I have to give a BIG thank-you to my friend and now business partner, Kamal Dorsey, for hitting the road with me on those long trips. Words can't express my gratitude and appreciation to you. And to you too, Andrea, because I know it's not always easy, but your support of our business venture means a lot. Big shout-out to NuWorle and Raheem! We're on the rise!

I have to thank one of the most respected and talented women in the publishing game right now, Dr. Maya Angelou. Auntie Maya, I love you for supporting me and standing by my side when others doubted your support of me. You can never know what that meant to me to have you host a book signing for me and endorse *Three Sides*.

I give a big thanks to Zane and E. Lynn Harris, two highly successful writers who have offered me support in one way or another. I appreciate the both of you.

I definitely have to thank Jonathan Demme for endorsing my script and supporting my writing. I am so honored and humbled to know you. Your love of New Orleans and your kind spirit have truly touched me. Thank you. And thank you again.

I most certainly can't forget Jedda Jones, Ms. Dupre, for her support and friendship. We will continue to put New Orleans on the map!

Willie Burton, Michelle Pitre, Abe Thompson, and Jackson Walker: Thank you for supporting my writing career and trying to help in your own way. I do notice and I'm very grateful.

I give a special-thank you to Rod 2.0 for supporting me from the beginning, and all the other bloggers, radio shows, and Web sites like Made In Brazil, Ms. Bev Smith, b.r. burns, Frederick Cooper, Bernard, Troy Johnson, aalbc.com, cushcity.com, Mosaicbooks.com, Delta Reviewer, SORMAG, Keith Boykin,

Jasmyne Cannick, and Nathan "Seven" Scott for the ads and shout-outs that helped me reach a wider audience. And all the bookstores and bookstore owners who carried my book and told readers to give me a chance. If I forgot somebody, please forgive me, but I thank you, too!

I thank the Lambda Awards for giving a nod to *Three Sides*. It was truly an honor and very humbling.

I have a BIG thank-you for Pam Walker, at page-turner, for the Web site and promotional tools that helped make me a success. Your patience and support of me during the tough times have not gone unnoticed.

I have to thank the lovely Carol Mackey at Black Expressions, for picking up *Three Sides* and giving me a chance. Thank you so much for your support.

I thank everyone at Broadway Books for believing in me. I miss all of you: Janet, Clarence, and Christian, who were there in the beginning. And I have not forgotten you!

Christine Pride, my new editor, who came on at the last minute and helped me see my story in a whole new light. Thank you, Christine, and I'm glad we're working together.

I have the most wonderful agent in the world. Manie Barron, what can I say but thank you, man. You came on when things were rough and you helped me get my business together. We're only just beginning! And to your business partner, Claudia Menza, thank you for coming on and helping me with the film aspect of the business. Both of you are great!

ACKNOWLEDGMENTS

The last thank-you, but certainly not the least, goes to all the book clubs, women's empowerment conferences, literary magazines, reviewers, black pride organizations, and mostly the readers who supported me. Without you—the readers—none of this would be possible!

TOO MUCH
of a GOOD
THING
AIN'T BAD

1

Sheila

"Straight, gay, bisexual, or whatever! Men are the masters at playing games. So why should I feel regretful about anything?" I said to Dr. Abney with a sinister look on my face, crossing one leg over the other. She became my therapist years ago when my marriage to Ken ended on bad terms. And here she was lecturing me on yet another relationship gone sour. "It is what it is."

"You're obviously hurt." She removed her eyeglasses and stared me in my eyes real intently. Dr. Abney was a pale white woman with gorgeous blue eyes and blond hair. Although she was a woman herself, at times Dr. Abney simply couldn't relate to my struggles being a dark-skin sister from the South. In fact, she didn't have a damn clue to the pain and suffering of being a black woman having to deal with these oversexed, immature black men who think they can do whatever the hell they want to, whenever they want to, regardless of who gets hurt in the process.

"In deep denial and repressing your true feelings about what happened." Dr. Abney continued with her psychobabble. I glanced at the clock on the wall. The time was three-thirty in the afternoon. I was now thinking about rush-hour traffic and how long it was going to take me to get across 395 out of Virginia to DC. The traffic situation in the nation's capital had to be one of the worst in the country. "This is never a good way to heal from a serious and painful ordeal like the one you've experienced recently."

I looked away from her, staring out the window for a moment. From Dr. Abney's office, you could see the Pentagon and the Washington Monument. A rush of power suddenly pulsated through my veins. The blood inside my body was warm. I felt myself smiling and saying, "I'm not repressed at all. Actually, I feel more liberated than I've felt in a long time. Revenge has never tasted so sweet."

After my relationship with Ken ended, I decided to never be one of those pathetic, weak women again. The kind of woman who wears her emotions on her sleeves. Loving a man so strong that I begin to lose myself. Putting his needs before my own happiness. Stooping to an all-time low and begging him to stay when I know he doesn't love me the same. That was me–Sheila Marie Doggett–forever heartbroken. That was all, of course, before I learned to play the game and get what I wanted on my own terms.

On my drive home that evening I thought to myself: Dr.

Abney was right about one thing, however. I was quite discontent and dealing with deep emotional scars for allowing myself to be entrapped in a game of foolish nonsense that was far beneath me. It was horrible how quickly things spun out of control and became utterly disastrous.

What happened was my best friend, Tiffany Evans, thought my life was in a crisis and decided I needed a stable relationship. A fresh start. After Ken, she said I had become bitter and angry. I was moving through one man after another without regard for the consequences. She called me everything but a whore to my face. But the rules of the game are often one-sided and unbalanced. Single men can date and sleep around as much as they like and never have to worry about risking their reputations.

Why can't women do the same?

I'm sick and tired of this double-standard bullshit. Men get to play the field while women are supposed to find one man and settle down. Hell, I tried the monogamous thing. Did what was expected of me. But where did it land me? I'll tell you: more confused than ever about black men.

We're told from adolescence that good girls don't sleep around; they save themselves for the right man. But somehow they forget to tell men the same thing.

So you grow up thinking you'll meet this one man—your Prince Charming—and the two of you will fall madly in love and live happily ever after. What a crock of shit. Most men, especially young men, aren't even interested in settling down with one woman. They're trying to get as much ass as they can get. Let's just be totally clear about this thing. I spent the greater part of my teenage and young adult years trying to make a relationship work with one man, and it always ended up with me in tears and heartbroken.

Things go well for a little while. He's so into me, we're almost inseparable. I'm the woman he wants to spend the rest of his life with. I make him wait months before we are even intimate. I think I'm playing it smart by making him wait. My hope is that he'll see me as a lady–special–different from the other women out there. The only problem is that while I'm waiting, he's getting his needs met by some other woman who isn't the least bit concerned about her clean reputation. Women like her make it real hard for good women like me. I honestly don't know if men can be faithful. I haven't seen it in my entire twenty-nine years on earth.

From the women in my family to my girlfriends, every woman that I've ever come across who is in a relationship has been misled by some lying, cheating man. Even my own mother went through an ordeal several years ago when she found out that my churchgoing, supposedly upstanding daddy was having an affair with a woman twenty years younger than he. You're talking about drama. My mother was left devastated. And, of course, my daddy was apologetic and regretful. Being their only child, I was placed smack dead in the middle of the situation. But we got through it somehow.

My mother eventually forgave him. At her age, she couldn't imagine starting over. I prayed to God that I would never end up like her: staying in a relationship with a man who cheated on me. The sad part about it was that I had always heard rumors about my daddy being a player and having his way with the ladies. Dr. Marshall Goodwin was a good-looking doctor with charm, money, and success. Women literally threw themselves at my daddy's feet for many years. He had just never gotten caught, until now.

But, anyway, Tiffany had supposedly picked out the right man for me: her husband's younger brother, Johnny. She told me he was good-looking and smart with long, manly arms and muscles. And the best part about it: he was from my hometown of New Orleans.

Of course, her descriptions of Johnny had my head spinning in circles. I hadn't dated someone from back home since I was in high school. If nothing else, I figured me and Johnny would have a lot in common and much to talk about given what had happened in the city with Hurricane Katrina last year. It was a difficult time and everybody's life was thrown into chaos. Johnny and his family were no exception.

Tiffany and her husband, Carl, fled the flood and moved in with me for a while along with Mother and Daddy. Johnny went to live with his aunt and uncle in Upper Marlboro, Maryland, about thirty minutes outside DC. I think for the first month after the storm hit, we were all simply in a state of shock given the enormity of the devastation at hand. Our beloved city was underwater. I still get goose bumps just thinking about it.

Tiffany and Carl lost everything, while Mother and Daddy were among the lucky ones. My parents lived in Metairie, on the outskirts of the city, and had only minor damage to their roof. However, they were definitely in the minority. There were so many other people suffering, and I was so disappointed with our government for its handling of the situation. There's no excuse for leaving Americans, taxpaying citizens, to fend for themselves for days during the worst natural disaster of our lifetime.

Don't even get me started. Weeks and months after Katrina, I was grouchy, angry, and could barely sleep thinking about my friends and loved ones in the city who couldn't get out. Katrina was a tragedy of monumental proportions, but it definitely put my life and priorities in perspective. What I was going through personally with men was nothing compared to what those poor people were dealing with in my city. No doubt, Katrina changed me in ways I can't begin to describe.

For instance, I left a high-paying VP position in educational publishing to go and work for a small management firm that oversaw the operations of at-risk schools in poverty-stricken sectors of DC. Working to improve the quality of life for young people was rewarding and enriching.

My job was to make sure that teachers and administrators did their jobs correctly. While most people had written off these kids from the inner city, my company, Advantage Principles, believed that every child was worthy of a quality, first-rate education regardless of their background or socioeconomic conditions. The standards were set high for everyone, including the parents of these kids.

Of course, everyone thought I had completely lost my mind, going from corporate America to managing schools in the "hood." However, money was no longer my motivation. I wanted to make a difference in the world and use my life for the greater good. Katrina showed all of us that nothing is guaranteed. We could be here today and gone tomorrow. And I was not going to waste another day of my life being unhappy and unfulfilled, especially with some man who didn't love or appreciate me.

When the storm passed so did the old Sheila. I was a new woman with purpose and meaning in my life. I know I must sound like a segment straight from the *Oprah Winfrey Show,* but the joy I had found post-Katrina was truly extraordinary. Something I wished everyone could experience in their own lives.

So, yes, I was a little skeptical about meeting this dream man given my rocky past and newfound independence. But Tiffany was my girl and I trusted her judgment. She knew me and what I was looking for in the opposite sex better than anyone. Therefore, I figured there was no harm in at least meeting the man. Right?

"I thought you would never get here," Tiffany said upon my arrival. Apparently, I had missed dinner, which I admit was rude. The truth was I had to force myself out of the house that evening. Thursdays were exclusively reserved for "me" time. I would come from work, soak in a hot tub, have a fabulous dinner, and watch *Desperate Housewives* with my vibrator underneath the covers.

Yes, I said it! Hell, when you're single, you get use to doing things by yourself and for yourself. I had no problems with being alone and taking care of my own needs.

"Girl, I'm so sorry. Got tied up at work," I lied, handing my jacket over to her and smiling. Tiffany was tall and big-boned with caramel skin and a gorgeous smile. She worked out at the gym relentlessly. Her arms were huge, too. I often told Tiffany she needed to pull back from lifting weights because she was losing her feminine qualities. I just don't get women who like working out and beefing up like men. Personally, I enjoy everything about being a woman, and there is nothing cute about pumping iron.

"It's okay. Come on in. Everyone is looking forward to meeting you." Tiffany took hold of my hand and walked me down a long hallway with huge paintings on both sides. One was of a black man playing a saxophone. The painting was so vivid and detailed that it felt alive.

Another piece depicted a black woman getting her hair straightened with a hot comb. It brought back memories of my childhood, sitting on the floor between Mother's legs and getting my own hair straightened with the hot comb. Moreover, walking down the hallway and gazing at all of those art pieces suddenly made me proud. Each piece captured some aspect of African-American culture—its richness and complicated history.

"Wow, I love the art," I said to her. "Every piece is so beautiful."

"Thank you. I'm glad you like them," said Tiffany as if she

had painted the pieces. But she was simply being her bubbly and kind self.

Tiffany was the type of person who rarely allowed life to get her down—one of the reasons why we remained such good friends over the years. No matter what the circumstances, Tiffany would find the good in the worst of situations. She believed that every good or bad thing that happens in a person's life is an opportunity to grow and expand spiritually. I was looking forward to finally meeting her extended family. Tiffany was my rock through the bumpy marriage with Ken, the court proceedings, and beyond. I couldn't have gotten through any of it without her. When all else failed, I joined the gym with her: not for lifting weights but to perfect my girlish figure, of course.

Working out at the gym was part of our regimen for a healthy mind, body, and spirit. Tiffany was actually the one who referred me to Dr. Abney for counseling. Although I would never admit it to her or my doctor, Tiffany was right about me needing therapy after Ken and I split. If nothing else, talking about my problems with a stranger was helping me to cleanse my system of negative vibes about Ken—about men period.

"Hey, everybody! Here she is." Tiffany walked me inside a dark room that was lit with candles. Her in-laws were a nice-looking, classy group of fine black folk who seemed poised for an evening of relaxation and spiritual enlightenment. They listened to jazz, sipped elegant wine, and ate caviar over light chatter. "Let me reintroduce you to everybody."

Tiffany started going around the room and pointing out everyone as if we were at an important board meeting with millions of dollars at stake. She was so serious and professional. "You remember my lovely mother-in-law, Mrs. Lomack."

I had actually met Mrs. Lomack at Tiffany and Carl's wedding many years before and always thought the woman was the epitome of femininity. Her hair was long and flowing; fingernails were neatly polished; a scarf was casually hanging off her shoulders. And her husband, Reverend Lomack, was as I remembered too—a distinguished-looking man dressed in a suit and tie with gray peppered in his mustache and low fade. The round frames he was wearing made him look more like a professor than the pastor of a megachurch.

Back in New Orleans, the Lomacks oversaw Mt. Zion Baptist Church—a congregation of over ten thousand members with a stadium, bookstore, and elementary school that could rival T. D. Jakes's Potter's House in Dallas. Although the Lomacks had lost their home and church in the aftermath of Katrina, they built a very comfortable new life in a plush neighborhood in Upper Marlboro. Yes, they had money, and it showed in every detail and piece of furniture inside the three-story estate with high ceilings and expensive artwork.

"And this is Mrs. Sabrina and her husband, Mr. Leonard," said Tiffany. Mrs. Sabrina was Mrs. Lomack's sister. She and her husband were real estate giants who had made a sizable fortune selling homes in a booming market in DC. White folks were moving back into the District and driving the property values through the roof. They actually sold Reverend Lomack and his wife their estate.

"I'm glad we finally get a chance to meet," Mrs. Sabrina said, flashing a warm smile and shaking my hand. After Katrina, she and Mr. Leonard took in Mrs. Lomack and the good reverend as well as several members of their extended family from New Orleans. And it was a big family! Mrs. Sabrina and her husband took care of everyone until they got on their feet. This was one family that had a lot of faith and unity that you simply don't see in many black families today.

The main reason Tiffany and Carl stayed at my house was I had only my parents to look after. You know, to give Mrs. Sabrina and Mr. Leonard some space to care for other family members. Needless to say, it was a crazy time in all of our lives, but we managed to get through it somehow. And I had been looking forward to meeting Tiffany's extended family, but our schedules could never match until now.

"She's such a pretty girl. Johnny is going to like this one," Mrs. Sabrina continued, her eyes surveying me like a hawk. I can't begin to describe how uncomfortable it was being the center of attention with all eyes on me. Hell, you would have thought I was the second coming to those people. They "really" wanted me and Johnny to meet. And I was beginning to wonder if something was wrong with this man. You know, like he had two heads, one leg, or something out of the ordinary.

"Oh, she would make a nice girlfriend for Johnny," an elderly lady in a wheelchair said from the corner of the room. She had a head full of white hair with chocolate skin like a Hershey's bar, and a dazzling smile that was fit for a Colgate commercial. She was Johnny's grandmother Eve. I had also met her briefly at Tiffany's wedding. "Where is dat boy, anyway?"

"You forgot, Mama? You sent him and Carl to the store to get you some vanilla ice cream," said Reverend Lomack. He was so charming and handsome, he reminded me of my own daddy—not the unfaithful side of him, of course. My daddy had some good qualities to him and being around Reverend Lomack made me appreciative of them.

Like Daddy, Reverend Lomack had a way of making everyone in a room feel special. He kept a pleasant smile on his face and would often make eye contact with you. I especially liked how Reverend Lomack was with his wife, though: so affectionate and genuine. He held her hand in his, stealing kisses from her like they were a pair of middle school kids. Without a doubt they were in love, and it was so cute.

"Well, they need to hurry up," Ms. Eve insisted, "so Johnny can meet our lovely guest. Why don't you take a load off and have a seat, sweetheart."

"Thank you, ma'am," I said. I eased in on the sofa next to Mrs. Lomack, who was sipping from her glass and smiling in my direction. She adjusted her scarf and crossed her legs. Mrs. Lomack had long, beautiful hair, and she often ran her hands through it. I sensed she was a humble, proud woman in touch with her inner self and womanhood.

Just looking around the room, I couldn't help but think of the Huxtables—*The Cosby Show* being one of my favorite sitcoms of all time. Like the Huxtables, these people represented the best of black America. And just like Bill Cosby's Cliff, Reverend Lomack and his brother, Mr. Leonard, were two of the finest gentlemen you would ever want to meet.

So, right now, I have to retract myself. There are at least a few good black men out there who are faithful to their wives and positive for our community. But Reverend Lomack and Mr. Leonard were also old-school brothers from back in the day when men knew how to treat women. They could definitely teach these arrogant, young black men out here today a thing or two about how to carry themselves with respect and dignity instead of walking around with their pants hanging off their waist and trying to be thugs for life. It literally makes me sick to my stomach when a man approaches me with his pants sagging, trying to be hard-core and gangster.

What's impressive to me and most "real" women is if you have a job, goals, and a loving relationship with your mother. Because if you treat your mother with respect and decency, then you'll know how to treat me in the long haul.

"So, Tiffany tells me you're in education?" asked Mrs. Lomack. She was now getting a gentle massage on the back from her husband. I also noticed that Mr. Leonard was stroking his wife's hand. These men loved their wives and they showed it. I could never get that kind of affection out of Ken. He was so emotionless, like a block of damn ice.

"That's correct," I said. "I work for a company that manages charter schools."

"Don't be modest," Tiffany said. "Ms. Lady here has helped

to turn some of the poorest-performing schools in the district into thriving stories of success."

Everyone clapped as if I were closing my final show on Broadway.

"That's impressive," Reverend Lomack said. "You see, all our young people need is a fair chance and opportunity and anything is possible. But it takes people like you who are willing to get out there and make a difference and give them a shot."

"I just do what I have to do," I responded modestly, although I was very proud of my accomplishments. Before I took the job with Advantage Principles, most of those kids were performing below the basic-skills level. The situation was pathetic indeed, but not hopeless. My plan was rigid, but effective.

I got rid of some of those lazy, lethargic teachers and hired new ones who were professional and cared about student learning. I also started a uniform program so those kids could focus on their education instead of the latest fashion trends. Moreover, I made their parents sign contracts with the school. If they were not actively involved in their child's education, then our academy wasn't the school for them. And I was very serious about this commitment from parents. They couldn't miss any parent/teacher conferences without a valid excuse. No one was getting off the hook when it came to bringing those kids to full potential.

Within a year, I saw major improvements. The students' attitude toward learning changed for the better, and there was even a slight increase in the school's overall performance on statewide tests.

"You know Johnny is in college," Ms. Eve pushed. "Education is something the two of you have in common."

"Mama, leave the girl alone," Reverend Lomack finally said. He must have sensed my uneasiness, or maybe it was the tight grin on my face.

"Speak of the devil." Tiffany greeted her husband, Carl, at the door with a warm kiss. Carl was a former college football player with broad shoulders and big arms. He was solid and masculine, but underneath that tough exterior he was a teddy bear at heart.

Carl was the type of guy who wasn't afraid to show his emotions. A while back, he and Tiffany had gotten into a huge fight over Tiffany's excessive spending habits. As a result, both their marriage and their finances were suffering. They even thought about separating. Carl found himself on my sofa with tears in his eyes. He wasn't bawling or anything, but he was very upset at the rift between him and Tiffany. After the incident, I realized how much Carl truly cared for Tiffany, and he has had my approval ever since.

"I didn't know I was missed," Carl joked with Tiffany. He noticed me on the sofa. "What's up, Sheila? I see you made it, huh? How you feeling tonight?"

"I've just been getting to know your wonderful family much better," I said. "Everyone is so nice."

"Where's Johnny?" Tiffany asked the question that everyone had to be wondering.

"Did someone ask for me?" Johnny glided through the door with a couple of bags in his hands, looking like he could be Morris Chestnut's twin brother. The man was every bit as fine and delicious as Tiffany had described. She had talked about Johnny's sex appeal on many occasions and her intentions were to bring us together much sooner, but the timing was never right. I thought we would meet at Tiffany and Carl's wedding, but the family said Johnny was away on important business. And when I asked Tiffany what business or company he was affiliated with, she ignored me. Hell, at the time I didn't push, but I was definitely curious.

Nevertheless, Johnny lived up to his sexy reputation. His teeth were perfect and that smile was radiant. Johnny had a toned body with silky dark skin that was so shiny and smooth it appeared to glow. His butt looked very delectable in those jeans, and I imagined him with his clothes off. You know, trying to get a fix on the size of the penis.

Hell, men see only one thing when they first meet a new pair of legs. I was only giving back what I had been getting all these years. Yes, indeed, I was already imagining having a lot of *fun* with Mr. Johnny.

"Come in, brother-in-law," Tiffany said, leading Johnny by the arm. "There's someone I would like for you to meet."

"Son, let me take those bags for you." Reverend Lomack took hold of the items in Johnny's hand and made a quick exit.

"Thanks, Dad." Johnny seemed very polite. His glow was magnetic. I tried not to stare. "What's up, peeps?"

"About time you get back here with my ice cream," Ms. Eve said. "I was beginning to worry some girl got hold of you out there."

"Come on now, Grandma." Johnny kissed her on the cheek. "You know you're the only woman for me."

Tiffany finally turned Johnny's attention toward me. "This my girl Sheila. She's actually an alum of Wheatley College, so I thought y'all should meet."

"Word," Johnny said. "I just started college there. What year did you graduate? I mean, it must have been last semester 'cause you don't look a bit over nineteen."

"I don't know about that." I blushed. Johnny was quite charming, like his father. "I actually graduated several years ago. Class of 1998."

"Word." Johnny seemed surprised. He was intelligent, but I also sensed a street-smart edge to him that was quite appealing. Although his family was obviously well-off, Johnny appeared to be a man with a complicated history. He was both an intellectual and a little on the rough side: a strange but interesting combination. "That's what's up."

"Don't be rude, son," Johnny's mother said. "Why don't you show Sheila around the place. I know she's dying to get from around us old folks."

"Not at all," I said. "You guys are wonderful."

Carl gave his brother a brush on the arm. And everyone was suddenly expecting Johnny to make the next move.

"You don't have to show me around." I stared at him. "I'm fine sitting right here."

"No, I insist." Johnny took hold of my hand. "Just follow me. I got you."

"The last man who said that to me," I joked, "ended up being my ex-husband."

"Word." Johnny smiled. "One man's loss can be another man's treasure."

Me and Johnny had immediate chemistry. There was definitely a connection between us. In fact, you would have thought Johnny and I had known each other for years the way we joked and carried on.

That night I found myself divulging personal information to him that often takes me months to share. I told Johnny everything about me and Ken, the divorce. I even shared details surrounding my parents' situation with Dad's younger woman. It was insane. I know. But Johnny felt like family already. Maybe it was my close friendship with Tiffany and her ties to Johnny's family, but talking to him felt natural and free.

Johnny told me a little bit about his past as well. He spent some time in prison for brutally attacking a man who was disrespecting his girlfriend at the time. His incarceration coincided with Tiffany and Carl's wedding. So that explained his absence and the "business trip" the family fabricated. Given the Lomacks' standing in the New Orleans community, I imagined Johnny's incarceration must have been a source of embarrassment for them. But what I respected about Johnny was that he wasn't dwelling on his past mistakes. While in prison, he obtained his GED and was now in college pursuing his dream of becoming a lawyer.

•   •   •

Two weeks later, I was sitting in my office at James Baldwin Academy and smiling. Johnny and I had gone on several dates and had spoken on the telephone every single day since our initial meeting. Things were certainly heating up, and I was really feeling him big time. I was even thinking about sleeping with this man, for God's sake, but then reality kicked me in the ass and came walking through my door, literally.

"Ms. Bitch, you may run things around this school, but you have crossed the line this time!"

When I looked up and saw James Santiago, one of our teacher's aides, standing in front of my desk, I had no idea of the reason for his anger. But we had had our problems, so I naturally assumed it was work-related.

From the time I arrived at Baldwin Academy, Mr. Santiago had been a problem for me. Since he was originally hired by the school's principal, Mr. Johnson, I had to walk a fine line. Mr. Johnson held Mr. Santiago in high regard and saw him as a major asset at the school. Mr. Santiago helped to turn around a class of troubled teens who were now more focused and excited about learning. I couldn't deny Mr. Santiago's contributions to the school, but it was his over-the-top antics that disturbed me.

I had a hard time getting Mr. Santiago to understand that Advantage Principles had rules and guidelines he had to abide by. He challenged my authority and made everything a battle between us. It was like the man was constantly testing me.

When I assigned Mr. Santiago to a particular class for the day, he would simply switch his schedule with another teacher's aide without my knowledge. On several occasions, I caught him using profanity with teachers, and he thought of many of the students as his friends. I couldn't get Mr. Santiago to understand the concept of student/teacher boundaries for anything in the world. Furthermore, the man couldn't distinguish the difference between men's and women's clothing and what's appropriate for the work environment. He wanted to wear high-heel pumps to school, and I simply wouldn't tolerate it.

Let me be totally clear about this, however. I have nothing against gay people, but I was not going to have Mr. Santiago sending the wrong messages to those kids. Women had specific dress codes, as did the students, and so did the men. Mr. Santiago went behind my back and told everyone that I had a problem with him being gay, which only added to the tension between us. Frankly, I couldn't stand him. And I'm sure the feeling was mutual.

"Mr. Santiago, what is the problem this time?" I asked him with an immediate attitude. He was the only person on earth who could evoke such strong negative feelings in me on the spot. "What is this about?"

"Don't act like you don't know." He leaned across my desk and stared me straight in the eyes. If looks could kill, I would be dead today. "I'm talking about Johnny!"

2

Johnny

Man, here we go again. Look like every time I take two steps forward, my ass knocked five notches backwards.

I might as well get straight into this thing, 'cause ain't no need of me cutting corners or trying to hold back on what happened. 'Cause I know how folks run their mouths, so you gone hear about what went down one way or the other anyway. All I can do is tell my side and you be the judge as to who was right or wrong in this situation.

Where should I start is the question.

I guess it starts with me wanting to pledge Gamma Phi Gamma at Wheatley College. Wheatley was one of the top black schools in the country. Like Howard University—our rival school—Wheatley opened up its doors to give black folks the same opportunities as white people. The college was named for Phillis Wheatley, a black woman writer from the eighteenth century. If you don't know who she is, look her up in the history books. Phillis Wheatley was one proud black woman who didn't let anything hold her down, especially the racism of that time.

A lot of my peeps went to Wheatley, so it was like I was continuing a tradition in the family. Even my Pops and Moms attended this college. They actually met on the campus and have been together ever since. And now their youngest was following in their footsteps.

You damn right I'm proud of that shit, man. I had been through a lot to get to that point in my life. Looking at me walk across that campus with a book sack thrown across my shoulders, you would never think my black ass had spent several years up in Sierra Leone—the state pen in Louisiana—for smashing some dude's head against concrete. It was over some petty shit, too. Me and that nigga had feelings for the same girl. You can say that was a low point for me. You know being locked up and caged like an animal. But it was in the pen that I made up my mind to one day go to college and become a lawyer. I was well on my way, too, and more determined to make it than ever. Although it seems when you're trying to move in a positive direction, you get all kind of negativity coming your way.

I had just started my sophomore year at Wheatley when Hurriance Katrina hit my hometown of New Orleans. Man, you're talking about some crazy-ass drama. Can you imagine your entire city being underwater? I'm looking at the TV and I can't believe my eyes what I'm seeing myself: dead people floating in the water, hundreds of folks stuck on rooftops. I was so worried sick out of my mind about my family and friends that I couldn't concentrate on school.

Thank God most of my peeps got out before Mayor Nagin called for a mandatory evacuation. Moms, Pops, my brother Carl, and his wife, Tiffany, came up to DC to stay with my uncle Leonard and his wife, Sabrina. My oldest brother, Ronnie, and his family evacuated to Texas. Man, we were separated all over the damn place. I had relatives who ended up in goddamn Utah, if you can believe. And you know ain't no black folks up there.

But the toughest part about all of this was worrying about my nigga James, who was stuck in the city days after the storm hit. That was one stubborn lil' dude who made up his mind to evacuate at the last minute and found himself in a whole lot of trouble as a result. He ended up in the Superdome with all of those thousands of other people living up in there like they were in a third-world country, man. James later told me that they barely had food and water and the smell up in that joint was so foul it was literally making people sick. He said folks were up in there passing out and shit.

I got really scared though when I couldn't reach James on his cell phone. All forms of communication were down and that was when the panic really set in for me that something bad could have happened to him. From the time the two of us connected up there in Sierra Leone, we had never gone a single day without talking to each other.

You have to understand. Despite all the bullshit, that's still my nigga. I do love that dude, man, even when we ain't seeing eye-to-eye on things. If it wasn't for James, I probably wouldn't have even gone to college in the first place. When James met me in the pen, I was a bitter and angry lil' nigga. I hated myself and felt like nobody understood my pain. You know like I was a lost soul out there in the world all by myself. Somehow, some way, James got to my heart though—broke through walls that I had built up for myself over the years.

To this day, I don't know how he did it. Maybe it was his realness that caught my attention. What you see with James is what you get. I like that about him. He ain't into playing games or trying to pretend to be something he's not. He'll tell you himself in a New York minute that "I'm gay, honey, and proud of who I am, baby. Take it or leave it." Yeah, my nigga keeps it real, but that ain't my swag by a long shot. Shit, I had spent most of my life pretending.

For the longest time, I couldn't accept that I was even attracted to dudes, let alone become intimately involved with one. My pops is a preacher, and I was raised in a strict family with Christian values, and I could tell you straight up that Pops or none of my people condone homosexuality. So being with James was a struggle from the beginning. It was hard loving him and trying to stay true to the values I was raised on as a child. Man, you don't know half of what me and James been through just to be together.

First, Pops tried everything he could to break us up, even going so far as bringing an old girlfriend of mine back in the picture—the same girl who I went to the pen for defending in the first place.

Tonya Thibodaux was her name. She was trouble back in high school and home girl was a beast when I came home from the pen. Tonya tried everything in her powers to get me. She had this fantasy of us picking up where we left off, which only fed into Pops's prayers that I wasn't into dudes. What a disaster that turned out to be.

Tonya found out about me and James and ended up blasting all my business to everybody in the hood. She had niggas trying to kill me. You know how ignorant folks can be, especially when they find out that you on some other shit—some gay shit.

To make a long story short, my bitch-ass cuz, Kojack, was one of those ignorant-ass niggas from the hood. He gunned down James inside Pops's church and left him for dead. For a hot minute, we didn't even know if James would survive the shooting. Kojack ended up in the pen for attempted murder while my family gathered around James in the hospital. When he finally pulled through, it was like our love for each other was even stronger than ever. So, you know if we got through all of that chaos, Hurricane Katrina for damn sure wasn't gonna stop us from being together.

Several days after losing my phone connection with James, I got a call from him that he was in DC at the airport. They evacuated the entire city, and he asked to be flown to the nation's capital to meet up with me. Man, you can't begin to know how happy I was that my nigga had made it out alive.

I rushed down to that airport and grabbed hold of him. We were hugging and kissing right there in the airport in front of all those people. That was the most open and out I had been in our entire relationship. Usually, I'm more reserved and low-key. Don't want people in my business. Just because I like kicking it with dudes don't mean I have to wear a badge for the entire world to see. Besides, that's only a small part of who I am. But James is different, and there lies the conflict between us.

Although I was happy to see James, me and him had a major beef from the beginning. He moved into my one-bedroom apartment and that was a mistake. When you live with somebody, you find out just how different you really are.

James was neat and anal. And a nigga like me was sloppy as hell. We argued about little things, like me leaving clothes on the floor and food on the table. Sometimes when the arguments got really out of hand, I had to remind James that he was living in *my* apartment. And you know that shit didn't go over well.

Before long, James thought I was trying to control him, which I'm man enough to admit was true. I'm not perfect by a long shot. I wanted James to tone things down a bit. You know, stop acting like a flaming queen all of the time.

Don't get it twisted, man. I accepted James for who he was and loved everything about him, but sometimes he was just over the top with his fashions and exotic hairstyles. That shit was embarrassing to me. Could you imagine walking down the street with a six-foot man sporting pink and blue hair and wearing high platform shoes?

The things I used to love about James in the pen started to turn me off in the real world. In the pen, I wasn't too concerned about James's image, because we were confined inside a close space. But on the outside, appearances matter a hell of a lot more. As much as we don't like to admit it, people do judge one another on what they see on the outside.

Man, you can't even get no job out here if you show up at an interview looking flamboyant. And James had a hard time finding a job, too. I was convinced that it had a lot to do with his overall look, but trying to get him to see things my way was like pulling a dead animal out of a lion's mouth. James had a mind of his own and was very strong-willed.

We eventually stopped communicating and we weren't fucking either. And once the sex goes bad in a relationship, it's pretty much over. Me and James started doing our own thing. I was focusing on activities at school and he was getting caught up in the gay scene in DC. While I'm busting my ass trying to study for a test in the wee hours of the morning, he's out at the Bachelor's Mill or the Delta Elite, two of several gay clubs in the District. Man, our lives were definitely moving in different directions. He had new friends I knew nothing about. And I was getting to know a whole new crowd of folks on campus.

During my sophomore year at Wheatley, I decided I wanted to pledge a fraternity—the same frat my Pops, uncles, and brothers are members of, so you damn right it meant a lot to me. James thought me pledging was whack though. He didn't understand why I would let somebody beat on me just to wear a couple of letters on my back. But like I tried to explain to him, there was more history and depth to frats than what he saw on the surface.

Gamma Phi Gamma was one of the oldest frats around town as well as the most respected. During the days of Jim Crow and racism, when there were few blacks attending college, brothers and sistahs came together on predominately white campuses in unity to preserve our legacy. Gamma Phi Gamma was a brotherhood that connected us in the struggle for our freedom and identity in a racist society that had no love for the black man. You heard me. The frat was about love for our people and culture and giving back to the community. That was my main motivation for wanting to pledge, and nobody was gonna stop me from getting my letters—not even James.

My brother Carl understood where I was coming from with the frat business because he had been in my same shoes. Carl pledged Gamma Phi at LSU several years ago. His wife, Tiffany, was a member of Phi Mu Phi, Gamma Phi's sister sorority. Since Carl and Tiffany felt where I was coming from, they introduced me to Sheila.

And contrary to what James thinks, Carl and Tiffany had no bad intentions in bringing me and this woman together. Sheila had graduated from Wheatley and was a member of Phi Mu Phi as well. If nothing else, Carl and Tiffany figured we would have a lot in common and she would be a great mentor to me. And they were right on the money.

Me and Sheila could relate to one another on so many levels, man. She had gone through the college experience and was now on the other side living and pursuing her dreams. Sheila was successful, man, and that was an inspiration to me. And although she had gone through a divorce and a lot of bullshit with her ex-husband, Ken, Sheila never wallowed in misery. I liked that about her, man. She often told me that no matter what curveballs life throws your way, you can't let it get you down.

I ain't gone lie, man. I wanted to get closer to Sheila—be that nigga she can depend on. Since Sheila had been hurt by several men in her past, she had a negative view of black men. I wanted to show her that we weren't all bad. There were some good brothers out there who respected and knew how to treat a woman. Getting closer to Sheila benefited me, too. She had a lot of contacts and knew some important people, especially up at Wheatley. A recommendation from Sheila and I was a sure bet to get into the frat.

Get this. Her cousin Reggie was the president of the under-grad chapter of Gamma Phi at Wheatley. How sweet was that? And without me even asking her, Sheila went out of her way to put me on with dude. Reggie was the man on campus and was very popular with the honeys, too. After Reggie took me under his wing, let's just say I had members of Gamma Phi calling and begging me to pledge their frat. Sheila had hooked my black ass up, and I couldn't have had it any better.

I ain't gone lie, man. Yeah, I found Sheila attractive, but I wasn't trying to use her to my advantage or anything. Well, maybe a little, but getting into a frat or any company or orga-nization is all about networking. I was simply playing my cards and trying to do something positive with my life. Instead of being out there on the streets selling drugs or something, I was trying to better myself by becoming a member of a frat whose mission was to uplift other black men. Me and Sheila simply found each other at the right time in our lives. We both needed one another for moral support on different levels. And it wasn't even all about connections like I said. Sheila was beautiful on the inside and outside, and I honestly enjoyed being in her company.

Sheila was a pretty, dark-skin sistah with long, coal black hair and a tight-ass body. She was shaped like a gymnast with big legs, a flat stomach, and nice round butt. Even though I was fucking around with James, my dick could still get hard for a beautiful woman. You can call it confused or whatever, but I'm just being as honest as I can be. Sheila got a nigga's dick rock-solid hard. I never said I was gay, anyway. Everybody else out there be trying to put a label on me. But I'm just me. Johnny Lomack from the mighty nine back in the NO.

After my experience with Tonya though, I definitely wasn't trying to get caught up in no bullshit either. I never misled Sheila into thinking we were gone be a couple or anything. To be honest, I just wanted to be friends with Sheila, because like I said she was a positive sistah to be around. On top of that, she was smart and was doing some good work in the community. One more thing we had in common: me and Sheila both understood the need to give back to those who are less fortunate.

What I liked most about Sheila though was that she never forgot where she came from. This woman had an MBA from Harvard and was now working with schools in the hood, trying to better the lives of kids who didn't have the best of opportunities in the world. What more can I say? Sheila was a good woman, and I don't feel guilty for wanting to be in her company either. But trying to explain that shit to James was like running into a brick wall. I remember the night everything went downhill for us.

• • •

"So, I see you finally made it home," I had said to James on his way through the door. The entire room was lit with candles and I had soft music playing. Dinner was warming on the stove. All of this was my attempt to recapture some of the magic between me and my nigga. "Why don't you come in and join me on the sofa."

"What is this about?" James asked with a skeptical look on his face. We hadn't had a romantic evening together in weeks.

"Can't I show my nigga some love?" I said, pouring him a glass of wine. James joined me on the sofa. He tried not to smile, but I saw him blushing. James had a beautiful smile, too. "You know I still love you, right?"

"Honey, I can't tell," James said, sipping from his glass. "Ever since I got up here in DC, you been treating a bitch like a stepchild, complaining about one thing or another."

"I know making these changes wasn't easy for you." I stared James in the eyes, admiring his new look.

After many arguments, James had finally given in to my demands and changed his entire appearance. Instead of the pink and blue hair, he was now sporting a bald head. James even got rid of his flashy clothes for jeans. The only thing he wouldn't give up were his handbags and pumps, which I was willing to live with.

"You know I appreciate you trying to make things work." I stroked James's chin, staring and thinking how gorgeous he was. Man, this dude looked better than some women I knew.

James had clear, soft skin and sexy, juicy lips like Angelina Jolie. "But you have to admit this new look did help you get that job."

"OK. I'll give you that much," James said, sipping from his glass and bopping his head to the music. I had some Wynton Marsalis on the CD player. "I do have a job now even though it's stressing me the hell out, honey."

"Tell your man all about it." I started massaging James's shoulders. You know, trying to get that nigga to relax, so I could put some wood on him. It had been a minute for me too, and I was looking forward to getting my freak on.

"Chile, where do I start?" James said. "It's that bitch again. I'm telling you, that woman is out to get me."

James had gotten himself a job as a teacher's aide at a charter school in southeast DC, one of the roughest areas in town. One of his friends knew the gay principal and he hired James on the spot. Some high-powered woman at the school had a problem with James being gay and was trying to get him fired; at least that was James's take on the situation. But I know my nigga, and he had a way of overdramatizing things.

"You can't be letting those people down at that school stress you out," I said, gently rubbing his feet. James had manicured toenails, too. No matter how much I tried to harden him up, James was one feminine-ass nigga and that was all there was to it. "Remember why you're there. To help those kids."

"You're right." James closed his eyes and took in the moment. I had finally gotten him to relax; his nipples were hard. I sucked on both of them like a newborn. "You always did know how to make me forget about my troubles."

I continued to massage his feet. "Maybe I should introduce you to my friend Sheila. She has a lot of pull with the school system."

James suddenly opened his eyes and jumped off the sofa like his ass had been bitten by a pile of ants or something.

"Sheila! Sheila who?" James hit the light switch and went ballistic. Man, this was the shit I couldn't stand about him. How he turned everything into a goddamn soap opera.

"First of all, calm your ass down," I said.

"Just tell me the bitch last name!"

"Doggett."

"Sheila Doggett is the woman you've been talking to on the phone and hanging out with?" asked James with so much anger in his voice that he could have popped a cap in my ass.

"Yeah, I told you about her."

"And she's the bitch who's been trying to get me fired at work," said James.

I was speechless. By the look on James's face, I had a feeling in the deep pit of my stomach that things were about to turn ugly between us—that this was going to be the beginning of a major shift in our relationship.

"How did the two of you meet again?" James pushed. Once he got started, there was no stopping him. "You better tell me the truth, too."

"I told you before," I said. "I met her through my brother. That's his wife's best friend."

"I should have known I couldn't trust your no-good-ass people!"

3

James

I'm a good person, y'all, and I really don't mean nobody any harm. I just need to get that off my chest right from the beginning, because I know how people are out here in this world, honey. I'm black, gay, and proud of who I am, and some people can't handle me being a straight-up, in-your-face type of person like Johnny's phony-ass people who are at the center of this controversy in the first place.

I don't understand why those people won't simply leave us alone. Me and Johnny love each other and have been through so much to be together, y'all, that it doesn't make any sense for us to be going through anything else. I was almost killed by one of Johnny's own cousins, honey. Shot me down like an animal in cold blood, but I survived, like a cat with nine lives.

You better believe I came back to Johnny after near death, so you know I ain't about to lose him now. I'll fight a bitch between two drops of rain for my man, honey, and walk through plates of hot iron and fire to be with him, too. I really want y'all to know how serious I am when it comes to my love for Johnny. So everything I tell you from this point on will make a whole lot of sense. I ain't even gone lie, y'all. I did some crazy shit trying to hold on to Johnny. So if you hear about me slashing somebody's tires, just know that it was love that made me do it. It was my love for Johnny, honey.

And I also would like to say up front that I'm very proud of Johnny and the fact that he's a college student and making something out of his life. I'm not jealous of him at all. Baby, nobody knows better than me how hard it is for black men out here. The world ain't trying to give a brother man nothing for free. You see, that's what makes what me and Johnny have so special. I understand him on a level like nobody else does, because we both been down similar roads. What I'm trying to say is that me and Johnny have done our share of time behind bars.

We ex-cons, honey. And right now it doesn't matter why I went to jail, but just know that I ain't going back for nothing in the world. I changed my life around and found God. Period. Nobody in this world is perfect, anyway. We all make mistakes, and I made quite a few in my time. But that's all behind me—behind us. Me and Johnny wanted greater things out of life. We often talked a lot about what our lives would look like once we got out of jail. One of Johnny's main goals was to get his GED and go to college. My baby is living his dream, honey.

As for me, I wanted to do something in fashion, because I'm a fierce designer and love the spotlight. Always could eat up a motherfucking runway, honey. Move over Tyra and Naomi,

James Santiago have y'all beat hands down. You don't have to believe me though. Just ask around the gay scene in New Orleans. I'm legendary, honey. You think Oprah's Legends Ball was a spectacle? Back in the day, all you had to do was stop by Club Circus in the French Quarter on a Wednesday night and there you would see me onstage giving them children—the gay boys and girls, honey—the performance of a lifetime.

Baby, I was serving them children drag, commanding attention every time I took to the stage. The children lived for me, and that's why I had so many enemies, too. When you got it going on, you gone get people hating on you. I've been stabbed and kicked around and bruised so many times that it ain't even funny. So what I'm saying is, I know firsthand that they have some cutthroat people out there in the world, and that brings me to Ms. Bitch, who sparked this beef between me and Johnny.

I'm talking about Sheila, commander in chief of Advantage Principles, a big corporation whose sole purpose is to steal government money under the guise of helping poor and underprivileged kids from the inner cities. Yeah, I said it, because it's true. That company didn't have a damn clue on how to go about reaching those kids from southeast DC, where I was a teacher's assistant. We were doing just fine, anyway, before they came with their principles and bullshit doctrines like the United States Army demanding and telling folks what to do.

Poor Mr. Johnson, the principal, didn't have a say in the matter either. James Baldwin Academy was a charter school started by parents, and they ran it with a closed hand and tight fist, honey. Although the parents felt Mr. Johnson was a good leader for the school, they also criticized him. Said Mr. Johnson was too timid and wasn't stern enough. But bottom line, the man was simply nice and genuine and people took his kindness for weakness. Mr. Johnson believed in giving everyone a fair chance, including me.

Personally, I think once word got out around the school that Mr. Johnson was one of the gay children, honey, heads began swirling and all of sudden he wasn't doing a good job as principal. And when Mr. Johnson hired me, that's when all hell broke loose around that school, honey. They thought he had completely lost his judgment for letting a wide-open punk walk the halls at Baldwin Academy, at least that's what I heard they said.

Baby, them parents and teachers were outraged at Mr. Johnson. They tried to pressure that man to give me my walking papers. Said I was not the right fit at the school and that I was giving the wrong impression to those kids regarding my sexuality. But the truth of the matter was, those kids loved me, and that was the real reason a lot of them teachers and parents up at the school hated me. They were jealous.

You should have seen me in action. I came in that school like the grand diva I am and got those kids together, honey. They assigned me to an English class with Ms. Greene, bless her heart. Ms. Greene was a sweet old lady who wore round frames and talked very proper like you would expect of an English teacher. Her class was supposed to be one of the toughest in the whole school. The rejects they were called: a bunch of knucklehead eighth graders who nobody wanted in their classes.

The problem with Ms. Greene was that she was too soft-spoken and she didn't command the kids' respect. With our kids—I'm talking about black kids, honey—you gotta go at them with authority in your voice and let them know who's the boss. I don't care what grade level or age they at, they are kids. Period. That meant no talking back to me or speaking without raising their hands to get my or Ms. Greene's attention. I told them from day one that they were at school to do their work and to take learning seriously. If they had a problem with the rules of the class, then I kindly pointed them to the door.

Of course, some of them tested and resisted me at first. Said I was not their teacher and that they didn't have to answer to me. I even had one boy called me a straight-up faggot to my face.

Shawn was his name and he was the class clown. He had everyone laughing at my expense. But, baby, I had been called worse, so it was not like he hurt my feelings or anything. I got up in Shawn's face, informed him that it didn't matter who I was screwing because that was none of his damn business. And whether he liked me or not, I was an authority figure at the school and he was going to respect me regardless. Moreover, if he thought he could beat my ass, then he was welcome to meet me outside and try.

Honey, those kids respected me as a result of keeping it real with them, especially upon hearing about me going to jail. I was honest with them about having been arrested for everything from fighting to stealing. I even showed them bruises and cuts on my body. And you could hear a pin drop in the room as everyone stared at me in shock, including Ms. Greene. After that incident with Shawn though, I never had a problem out of one of those kids. They not only respected me for keeping it real, but saw me as someone who understood where they were coming from being teenagers.

The problem with a lot of teachers and administrators today is that they can't relate to these kids because they're so busy trying to talk down to them. Our kids are intelligent and advanced beyond their years. Chile, you can't be talking about the birds and the bees with them these days. You gotta tell kids about how fucking without condoms can get their asses caught up with HIV. You know what I mean?

Like I said, I kept it real, and within a month I had become a favorite around the school. Some of those kids called me Ms. J and others referred to me as Mr. Santiago. It didn't matter what they called me as long as they addressed me with respect.

And, honestly, I adored those kids. Gave that job one-hundred-plus percent. I spent a lot of time counseling kids with their problems and many of them became my friends. When they had a problem with one of their peers or a serious issue going on at home, they came to Ms. J for advice. You would not believe some of the things I heard from those kids, too. Abuse. Drugs. Sex. You name it. They were dealing with some serious shit both at school and at home.

Anyway, two months at the school, and here comes Ms. Bitch, Sheila Doggett, and her entourage, white business execs who had a vision of taking the school in the hood to new heights. But it was bullshit that I smelled a mile away. Advantage Principles received millions of dollars from the government to help disadvantaged schools, but we never saw a dime of that money. They couldn't have cared less about those kids, and Ms. Bitch was the biggest joke of all.

Sheila was a bourgeois black girl who grew up with a silver spoon in her mouth and was now trying to do some good in the hood. But she was being used by Advantage Principles as a token. Sheila was the only black in the entire company, and they assigned her to the poorest school in the worst neighborhood in DC. What I didn't like about Ms. Bitch was that she got up in my face her first day on the job.

All of sudden I couldn't wear pumps or carry purses or anything that made me look like a woman. Ms. Bitch said that I was unprofessional and too friendly with some of the kids, particularly the male students. She was suggesting that something inappropriate was going on, which was totally out of line. Just because I'm gay, she assumed that I messed around with little boys. Ms. Bitch was ignorant and that was all there was to it. She had no idea who I was or what I had accomplished at that school, and didn't give a damn either. Ms. Bitch and Advantage Principles were all about appearances and grandstanding for the public.

Before long though, Sheila took center stage and Mr. Johnson faded into the background. Advantage Principles, with Ms. Bitch's guidance, started a uniform program and turned our kids into robots. They had to march down the halls in a single-file line, as if they were in boot camp or something. We had to teach them lessons that were already scripted, and the kids gave their answers in unison.

Furthermore, they couldn't run or throw a football on the playground. What kind of school doesn't allow students to actually play at recess? Suddenly, Baldwin Academy resembled something out of 1940s Germany when Hitler was in power. Of course, I couldn't take it, so I voiced my opinion to the charter board. I told those parents—in front of Ms. Bitch's face—that Sheila and Advantage Principles were doing the school a great disservice. That the kids had become unhappy and showed much apathy toward learning. Ms. Bitch took my statements as a direct slap in the face and vowed to get rid of me, somehow. And the flames were ignited.

When I found out that she and Johnny had been hanging out, I was outdone, honey. Couldn't believe that Johnny's brother and entire family were in on the scheme. I was hurt and never felt so betrayed in my life, especially by Johnny. He refused to see the situation from my position. Said I was overreacting and being melodramatic.

Sheila was supposedly introduced to Johnny for the sole purpose of being his mentor. She had attended Wheatley in the mid-nineties and was a member of a sorority. Once Johnny got to college, he wanted to pledge, too. He saw Sheila as his way into the fraternity. You see, her cousin ran the frat at Wheatley. And the only way Johnny could get into Gamma Phi whatever—that was so important to him—was to go through this guy.

To be honest, I don't give a damn what Johnny's reasons for hanging out with Ms. Bitch were. When he found out that this woman—who he had become close friends with—was the same bitch who was trying to destroy me at work, Johnny should have stood by my side and ended their friendship. Period. But he defended her instead. Spit in my damn face. Johnny had the audacity to suggest that I was jealous of him for being in college and wanting to pledge.

First of all, I had no problem with Johnny desiring to pledge a fraternity that his father and brothers and uncles were members of. I just thought it was a bunch of foolishness for someone at his age. Mind you, Johnny was pushing thirty and most of the kids who were pledging him were nineteen and twenty years old. I couldn't understand why he would let some teenagers whip his ass for the sake of wearing a bunch of letters on his back that don't mean a damn thing in the real world.

But the biggest problem was: Johnny was changing toward me. The things he once loved about me, Johnny now couldn't stand. He made me cut my long hair. Clip my fingernails. You see, he was trying to project this image to everyone on campus of being straight and hard-core. Johnny said he would never make the fraternity if anyone found out that he was gay.

As a result, he started seeing me as a threat to his overall goals while Sheila was held in high esteem. She served a greater purpose of helping him get what he wanted. Ms. Bitch was only his cover. Part me felt sorry for Sheila, because deep down I knew Johnny was only using her to get into that fraternity. But whatever the reason for them getting closer, I still didn't like it. It didn't feel good to see my man spending so much quality time with someone other than me. Johnny may have been willing to do anything to pledge that fraternity. And I was willing to do whatever I had to do to save our relationship, honey.

So, you damn right I confronted Ms. Bitch at school about her involvement with Johnny. Told her straight up that Johnny was mine and that she better back off. Ms. Bitch turned it around and told Mr. Johnson and the charter board that I had threatened her life. Like I said, this woman would have done anything to get rid of me and she tried her hardest.

I went into a deep depression, honey. Felt so alone being miles away from home—from Flo, who had always backed me up no matter what. Although she was my mama, Flo was more like my friend. I could depend on that girl whether I was right or wrong in a situation. You know nobody can love you like a mother.

Me and Flo got separated after Hurricane Katrina though. She went by some of my people in Texas and I came to DC to be with Johnny, who had just started school at Wheatley a month before the storm hit. Katrina was a hot mess, honey. Baby, I'm still fighting Ms. FEMA for my coins. But that's another story for another day.

Flo begged me not to go to DC, too. Her famous last words were: Them people don't love you. Flo was referring to Johnny's family, who had done any- and everything in the past to keep us apart. But bringing Ms. Bitch into our lives was the last straw, and I wasn't beyond letting them know how I felt either.

"I need to speak with Tiffany and Carl," I immediately said to Mr. Leonard at the front door. He was wearing eyeglasses and holding the Bible in his hand. Mr. Leonard probably was studying the Bible with Reverend Lomack. Johnny told me that his dad and Mr. Leonard were very close brothers. Both of them were very involved with the church, too. But the occasion of my visit was no religious matter, honey. I had come to kick somebody's ass for getting in my business and causing problems between me and Johnny.

"Is everything okay?" asked Mr. Leonard in a soft voice. He was pleasant and warm and always hospitable when I was in his presence. I really can't say anything bad about the man or his wife, Mrs. Sabrina. They are good people and truly blessed, honey. And both of them got that paper. They are big-shot real estate brokers, so they couldn't help but be swimming in dollar bills.

"Not really," I said with a straight face and major attitude. "I have something I need to get off my chest!"

"Why don't you calm down?" he said.

"Oh, I'm calm," I said, pushing my way through the door. "I just need to speak with Tiffany and Carl."

"Well, they are not here at the moment," he said. "Maybe there's something I can help you with."

"Leonard, what's going on in here?" Johnny's dad, Reverend Lomack, walked in on us. He must have heard the commotion. "And, James, what are you doing here this time of night?"

"The great Reverend Lomack," I toyed with him. "I see you up to your old tricks again. But it's not gonna work. You see, me and Johnny, we love each other. So deal with it."

"Excuse me," he said, raising his voice. Started approaching me. Reverend Lomack was a tall man with broad shoulders and a mean stare. He could scare the hell out of you without saying a single word, but I was definitely "time enough" for his ass. My mama, Flo, always said, "The bigger they are, the harder they fall, honey."

"Excuse my ass," I said. "You know exactly what I'm talking about."

"Keep your voices down and show some respect in this house," Mr. Leonard said as he got in between us. "People are sleeping. Besides, we're all adults here."

"Tell him that," I said, biting words between my teeth and holding back tears. "You and your son have gone too far this time. Introducing Johnny to some woman. I was such a fool to believe that you people would ever accept me!"

After Hurricane Katrina caused so much suffering in our lives, I thought things were really gonna be different between me and Johnny's family. There had been a great deal of loss and devastation on all of our parts. This was supposed to be a time of healing and coming together. I loved Johnny's entire family as if they were my own blood. Shit, I even had some of Reverend Lomack's blood running through my veins.

When I was shot by Johnny's cousin, I lost a lot of blood that was a rare type. Johnny's dad was a perfect match. Reverend Lomack saved my life, and I couldn't help but love him afterward. I just thought he and the family felt the same about me, too. I guess I was wrong. Some people's minds you can't change regardless.

"I think you should leave before we both say something we regret later," Reverend Lomack said. He was holding the front door for me to leave. "We'll talk about this situation at another time when we're all much calmer and thinking clearly."

"Whatever," I said on my way out. "Y'all people ain't worth my damn time, anyway."

Reverend Lomack slammed the door in my face. Driving home, I was clutching the steering wheel and shaking. My nerves were so bad, y'all, that I was speeding across the highway and driving like those white bitches Thelma and Louise, who drove off the cliff in that movie. But this was no suicide attempt, honey. It was simply bad nerves. My heart was racing and pounding against my chest. A call from Johnny on my cell phone that evening didn't help matters either.

"I'm on my way home. What do you want?" I said upon answering the phone.

"My pops just called me," Johnny said with a raw tone in his voice that scared me out of my wits. We've had our share of arguments over the years, but nothing of this magnitude. Johnny sounded like he suddenly hated me and that was a weird feeling. "And now you've gone too far. Almost attacking Sheila at the school and now confronting my people with this bullshit?"

"So, you defending that bitch to me?" I screamed into the phone, pulling off the road. The pains in my chest had gotten so bad so that I could hardly drive. "What about my feelings?"

"Your shit will be waiting for you at the door!" Johnny shouted before hanging up.

I could hardly catch my breath.

4

Sheila

The last thing I wanted was to make a scene in front of everyone, but Tiffany left me no choice. She had been avoiding my calls and dodging me at every turn. So, when I saw her lifting weights on the main floor of the gym, I seized the opportunity to confront her face-to-face regarding Johnny.

Tiffany and I had gone through so much together over the years, and this growing rift between us was extremely uncomfortable. This was the woman whose shoulders I had cried on after Ken and I split and who I had shared some of my deepest secrets with. But the love and the support worked both ways. I had seen Tiffany through the tragic loss of her only brother. He died in a head-on collision with an eighteen-wheel truck. It was a tough time, but we got through the tragedy with faith and friendship.

Then there was the breast cancer scare. Thank God that

turned out to be benign. The lump was successfully removed without Tiffany having to lose her whole breast. The point being was that I was there for her, sitting in the doctor's office for hours, holding her hand and waiting on the damn test results. It was excruciating to think that my girl might have cancer–that I could actually lose her to that awful disease. I think I was more nervous than she was. But the celebration was even more special and memorable. We went out to B. Smith's in Union Station for drinks and dinner upon hearing the good news from the doctor.

After that incident, Tiffany and I became almost inseparable. She wanted to cherish every moment together. The thought of dying from cancer made Tiffany appreciate life–and her friendship with me–even more if that was possible. We hung out just a little bit more often than usual. We shared dinners and conversations about clothes and men and life. Tiffany knew my joys and my greatest hopes for the future. But above all, she knew what kind of man I wanted in my life, and it for damn sure wasn't someone like Johnny. And that was why I couldn't fathom her reasoning behind introducing me to a gay man. Hell, I know I had gone through some bumpy relationships and had a long dry spell without getting laid. However, for her to think that I was desperate enough to take a man who was sleeping around with other men was mind-boggling to me.

How Tiffany could justify this decision of hers was beyond me, but I for damn sure wanted some answers.

"Sheila!" Tiffany's body lay flat across the exercise board; arms suspended in the air with several hundred pounds of weight above her head. She was surprised to see me, because it was early in the afternoon. At that time, I was usually at work.

"Where's Greg?" she asked, looking for her trainer.

"He had to run," I said with a wicked grin on my face. "So I guess you're stuck with me."

Greg, who had been spotting her, had stepped aside and allowed me to take over without Tiffany even realizing it. I had come up from behind him with my finger pressed against my lips, being really sneaky and calculating.

"Are you just gonna stand there?" she asked, struggling with the weights. "Give me a hand, damn it!"

I stood over her with contempt in my eyes, thinking this was indeed the perfect punishment for her betrayal. Tiffany prided herself on being outrageously fit. She often bragged about the large amount of weight she could lift and how she was stronger than most men. Her muscular body was a showpiece, but even Tiffany had a breaking point. She had already lifted several sets in the air and was simply burned out. As she tried to place the weights on the rack behind her, Tiffany's entire face turned red and she never looked more vulnerable. At any moment, those weights could have collapsed on top of her.

"You're lucky I'm not evil." I finally assisted her in placing the weights on the rack. It was a struggle for both of us, but we managed. Of course, I was more concerned about breaking a nail than showing off my strength.

"Are you crazy?" She stood up, gasping for air.

Folks stared in our direction. It was in the middle of the day at Bally's, and the room was flooded with men and women of all ages. DC had a large population of gay black men, and Bally's at Twenty-third and L streets seemed to be a meeting place for them. They were all over that gym, flaunting their bodies. I had actually seen men exchange numbers at the gym.

As a single black woman, I couldn't help but wonder about my prospects of meeting a decent straight brother. Getting to know Johnny—no matter how brief it was—made me fearful of the dating scene altogether. And I had my best friend to thank for bringing this man into my life. So of course I was furious with her.

"What is your problem?" Tiffany said to me as she held her neck to make sure it was still attached to her body. She stared at me in disbelief. The kind of look that someone gives a person who's acting out of character and showing a darker side of herself. "You could have killed me."

"Don't be so damn dramatic," I said, keeping my voice to a whisper to avoid attracting any more attention toward us. "If I wanted you dead, believe me it wouldn't be hard given how I'm feeling right now."

"You're obviously not in your right state of mind, so I'll talk to you later." Tiffany grabbed her water bottle and towel off the floor. She was preparing to leave, but I wasn't finished with her yet. I blocked her from passing me.

"How could you set me up with a gay man?" I said, trying to hold in my anger and keep from screaming. It took a great amount of self-control.

"Johnny is a nice guy." The expression on Tiffany's face spoke volumes. She was obviously ashamed, avoiding eye contact with me. "Carl thought you might be able to help him."

"Help him?" I frowned. "How in the hell can I help him if he's gay? So Carl put you up to this?"

"He doesn't think his brother is gay." Tiffany defended Carl's actions as well as her own. "Just needed the right woman to make him see the way."

I shook my head in utter disbelief. Just couldn't believe what I was hearing. But, honestly, I wasn't really *that* surprised. Although Tiffany is a strong woman physically, she can be weak-minded. I know I had said that Carl truly loved Tiffany—and that I had admired him for his love of her—but he wasn't perfect by a long shot. Carl had a controlling side to him, but he was not God. And thus he had no business sticking his nose into my personal life. No man controls me, but that's how he treats Tiffany. He could literally get her to do anything.

Carl is a big freak, and one time he actually persuaded Tiffany to allow another woman into their bed for a threesome. Although Tiffany was totally uncomfortable with the idea, she went along with Carl because that's what "he wanted." Like I said, the girl doesn't have a mind of her own.

"I think you would jump in a deep ocean," I said, "if Carl told you to do so. When are you going to stop letting this man control your every move?"

"I'm not listening to this again." Tiffany clutched the water bottle, pointing it in my direction. "Besides, we were trying to look out for you. It was not our intention for anyone to get hurt. We love you, sweetie."

"What a bunch of bull!" I yelled in her face. Tears welled up in the corners of my eyes. Tiffany looked pitiful. "You used me in the worst possible way."

Don't misunderstand me though. I wasn't hurt because Johnny turned out to be gay. Hell, I was used to men disappointing me. What I couldn't get past was the fact that my best friend in the whole world would put me in this type of situation in the first place. Even if I was lonely and bitter after Ken and I split, Johnny Lomack was not the answer to my prayers. That man represented a segment of society that I, and most women, loathe with contempt—men who sneak around with men and hide their sexuality from unsuspecting women.

Tiffany seemed like a total stranger to me. Not someone who I had shared most of my adult life with. Hell, maybe I was overreacting and being a little melodramatic, but she deserved every bit of it. Best friends are supposed to keep you out of trouble, not place you in the middle of drama.

"I mean, do you get some perverted pleasure seeing me stress?" I stared at her real hard, thinking about all those times I had actually cried on her shoulders. Maybe Tiffany enjoyed seeing me weak and vulnerable. You know, I didn't really know what to think, so I was pulling information out of the sky at this point. "For you to think that I would want to fool around with some gay man."

A young, feminine guy glided by us with a smirk on his face. This was not your typical dialogue for the gym, and I imagined after our occasional outbursts folks were eavesdropping on our conversation. He, along with everybody else, was getting an earful that afternoon at Bally's.

"First of all, I can't believe you're asking me that," Tiffany said, wiping sweat off her forehead. "You know I want nothing but the best for you."

"I thought I knew you," I said, "but now I don't know what to think. You must feel I'm desperate or something."

"Of course not, sweetie." She reached out to touch my arm. I pulled away from her. "I think you're blowing this way out of proportion. Let's go somewhere and talk about this."

"Thanks to you, Johnny's insane boyfriend tried attacking me at work," I gritted words between my teeth. "You see what type of mess you've put me in?"

"Johnny told us what happened," she said, "but don't blame him. It was all me and Carl. And I'm so sorry, Sheila."

The worst part about this situation: I had to deal with Johnny's lover, James Santiago, who was downright trifling, and to be tied to him in any way outside of the confines of Baldwin Academy was far too much for my taste. His bad attitude and violent tendencies made me very uneasy. When James showed up in my office the other day, threatening me, I was afraid for my life.

"I love you," Tiffany said, choking over her words. "I never meant to hurt you."

"I have nothing more to say to you," I said without remorse. "Enjoy your workout."

The next day, I was still reeling from my fight with Tiffany. I had decided enough was enough with Tiffany, Johnny, James, everyone.

"I would like for this man to be terminated effective immediately," I said. I was on a rampage that only continued and intensified at work. "That's my recommendation."

James and I sat in front of Mr. Johnson, who had been away at a leadership conference for principals and was now getting all of the gory details firsthand. The tension inside that room was so thick it could have been cut with a razor blade.

"Terminated for what?" shouted James. He stared directly at me with such hatred in his eyes that it made my stomach churn. I have never in my life felt so uncomfortable around an individual. From his flamboyant and outrageous clothing to his loud, obnoxious insults, this man made my blood boil.

"This is personal," he continued. "You mad all because I told you to stay away from my man and I had every right to."

"First of all, you should tell your man to leave me alone," I fired back at James. The look on his face was priceless, as I stung him with the bitter truth. "Since he's been blowing up my phone every time I look up."

And for the first time, James was speechless. He really cared about Johnny and the hurt expression on his face proved it. That weirdo actually has feelings, I thought to myself. But

James's emotions were the last thing I was concerned about at the moment. The only thing I wanted was to put this awful situation behind me. I had already cut Johnny out of my life, and I wanted this weirdo gone for good, too. James's unprofessional behavior toward me only proved my point that he was not a good role model for our students.

"Mr. Johnson, I hope you understand this is nothing personal against Mr. Santiago," I expressed with sincerity, "as he's suggesting today."

Mr. Johnson ignored us, writing something down in a yellow notepad. He was also a gay man, and the last thing I wanted was for him to believe James's assertion that I was homophobic. At this point, however, Mr. Johnson was hard to read, and I couldn't tell if I was getting through to him or not.

Hell, I don't have a problem with gay people as long as they stay out of my way and don't cross the line. What I particularly liked about Mr. Johnson was that he was very conservative with his lifestyle. He didn't put his business or sexuality in everyone's face, which I totally respected.

But James was a different matter. He wanted to be a woman, and something about his intentions bothered me. Let's just say he was too much to handle at once, and therefore I was not going to shed a single tear in his absence.

"Yeah, whatever. You always had a problem with me, anyway," retorted James. "So I'm not even surprised."

"You think what you like," I said, "but this is not about you and me. It's about what's best for these kids."

"And I'm not, Ms. Bitch?" he yelled. "I care about these kids with all my heart, too!"

"Okay. I've heard enough," Mr. Johnson interjected. He placed his pen down on the desk and stared at both of us real intently. "The two of you are adults here and you will conduct yourselves as such."

"You need to tell her that." James jumped out of his seat, pointing at me. He was belligerent and beside himself with anger. I braced myself for a possible physical confrontation. "Can't you see she hates me?"

"Sit down, Mr. Santiago!" Mr. Johnson said with authority. Since he was a short, timid man with a soft voice, it was quite startling to hear him raise his voice. "Before I have you removed from the premises."

James immediately plopped down in the chair and crossed his arms, pouting like a two-year-old.

"I have heard both sides of the situation," Mr. Johnson continued, "and, Mr. Santiago, your behavior here today and toward Ms. Doggett is unprofessional and completely unacceptable."

"But—" James started, but Mr. Johnson cut him off.

"But nothing," said Mr. Johnson. I sat with my legs crossed, staring straight ahead as if James was suddenly not even in the room. "Whatever personal problems you have with Ms. Doggett, this school is not the place for it."

Mr. Johnson opened a folder on his desk and placed his signature on a couple of documents. "I am going to honor Ms. Doggett's recommendation."

Of course, I had to contain my emotions and try to force

myself not to smile. This was a day I had dreamed about from the moment I'd laid eyes on James. But I wasn't coldhearted. There was a small part of me that felt sorry for him, especially after seeing that devastated look on his face.

"So, you gone fire me just like that?" he asked. "After all I've done for this school?"

Mr. Johnson looked up from his papers. "If you would stop interrupting me, Mr. Santiago, I could finish what I was saying."

"I'm sorry, sir." He sounded like a totally different person. James was kissing Mr. Johnson's ass and that was blatantly obvious. "Go right ahead. You're in charge."

"I'm not going to terminate you permanently," explained Mr. Johnson. I balled my fist underneath the chair. "However, you will be suspended for a week without pay. Now, if you will please excuse me, I need to speak with Ms. Doggett alone."

"Thank you so much, Mr. Johnson," James said on his way out the door. He was quite relieved, but I was pissed beyond measure.

"You're making a big mistake," I immediately said. "What is it going to take for you to see that man is dangerous and volatile?"

Mr. Johnson grabbed his yellow notepad and stood up to leave. Every morning he walked the entire grounds of the school. "I know you're disappointed, but there was not enough concrete evidence to fire him. We would be looking at a lawsuit."

"If I can speak frankly, Mr. Johnson." I stood in front of his desk and looked him straight in the eyes.

"Please do," he said.

"Your charter board hired my company because you wanted results," I said. "And my leadership has taken this school to new heights."

"And I appreciate what your company has done for the school," said Mr. Johnson. "But wearing female apparel is not sufficient grounds to terminate a man's employment. No matter what you think of him, Mr. Santiago is one of the best teacher's aides at this school. He's done so much to help turn Ms. Greene's class around. Now, we both have work to do and a school to run. Good day, Ms. Doggett."

Mr. Johnson left me standing there in his office upset and with bitter feelings. Getting James out of this school was now more personal than ever. His presence would only be a constant reminder of Johnny, and I really wanted to erase any memories or associations with the both of them. Hell, if you can imagine, all of this was completely embarrassing for me. Since James had a big mouth, some of the teachers were already aware of our conflict.

"Reggie." I held the phone up to my ear. His call couldn't have come at a better time. "I was just about to contact you."

"What's up, cuz?" he asked. "You sound kind of down."

"We really need to talk, Reggie."

5

Johnny

"Just be yourself, son," Pops said to me. Me and him, along with my uncle Leonard, stood outside Wheatley's auditorium, where the members of Gamma Phi Mu prepared to host their annual smoker.

It was a cold winter day, and about fifty well-dressed brothers waited nervously to enter the building. We all knew that half of us probably wouldn't even make the line, because Gamma Phi was very selective. Besides good grades, you had to have the right personality and swag to become a member. Man, I was just glad to have my pops and uncle there supporting me. They had gone through this process many years ago, and now it was my turn to take the torch.

"And remember, most of this is a mind game," Pops continued, fixing my tie and dusting off my blue suit. It reminded me of being five years old, when Pops dropped me off at school for the first time. I could recall being anxiously excited and fearful of the unknown at the same time.

"I want you to take this." Uncle Leonard handed me a Bible that was so old the pages inside of it were falling apart. "Our dad, your grandfather Joe, gave this Bible to me when I was a student in college. I had just become a member of the frat."

"Thanks, Uncle Leonard." We hugged tightly. "Man, I don't know what to say."

"Just always keep God first," he said, "and everything else should be added unto you."

"You okay, son?" asked Pops. He must have sensed how nervous I actually was. Man, I couldn't keep still for nothing in the world. Shit, it was cold out there, and the adrenaline was pumping through my body. I had so many damn thoughts running through my head, man.

This moment was so much bigger than me. Growing up, this was all Pops and his brothers talked about—their sons going off to college and one day pledging Gamma Phi. You don't know how many stories Pops and my uncle had told me about joining the frat. This was their dream come true for me. Don't get me wrong. I was excited, too, but it was their energy that kept me going from the beginning.

What I'm trying to say, man, is that pledging a frat meant I had to go back in the closet. You know, I had to be more secretive than ever about my sexuality. If anyone suspected I was gay, there was no way in hell I would ever make the line. Brothers don't be down with that gay shit, and I knew coming into this situation that it wasn't gone be easy. But I had to try, man–for my Pops. The smile on his face and that look in his eyes made me feel accepted and loved by him. And one thing about me and Pops: we haven't had too many special, tender moments in my adult years. Spending time in the pen made me the black sheep of the family. By going to college and pledging Pops's frat, I was hoping to turn my image around in his eyes. Become the man that Pops always dreamed that I could be.

"Are you sure you're okay, son?" Pops asked again. "You look a little scared to me. What do you think, Leonard?"

My uncle stared me in my eyes and smiled. They were both messing with me, man. "Yep. He looks scared to me. I don't know if he's ready for those burning sands."

"Man, I'm good," I said, rubbing my hands together to generate some heat. "I ain't scared of nothin'. In fact, y'all can take off."

"Just remember what I said," Pops said before bouncing. "It's all a mind game."

"And keep God first," Uncle Leonard added. They were the ones acting nervous, in my opinion. You know, the way they kept repeating themselves. "And everything will be added unto you."

"Go, man," I finally said to them. "I'm good. Thanks for coming."

After Pops and Uncle Leonard bounced, I joined the line outside the auditorium and immediately ran into Steve, who was in my Intro to Law class. We were surprised to see each other.

"What's up, dude?" Steve greeted me with a handshake and wide smile. He was a fair-skinned cat with a low fade. Steve was also about six-four, and his height afforded him the distinct title of All-American. Steve was one of the best basketball players at the school. Although I had admired his game on the court, I'd never spoken to him until now. In class, we would nod at each other and that was the extent of our interaction.

"Man, just trying to stay warm," I said, avoiding eye contact with him. Steve was attractive to me, and the last thing I wanted was for him, or anyone for that matter, to figure out my status. Like I said, it would be disastrous if someone realized that I fucked around with niggas. So I made an extra effort not to look Steve straight in the eyes. "And get my mind right for this process."

"I hear you, dude." Steve sounded like a white boy, but he was a cool cat. I had seen him with some of the prettiest sistahs on the yard, which made him a sure bet to make the line. Gamma Phi Mu was known for hosting parties and attracting some of the hottest chicks on campus. And if you could bring some of your swag to the frat, that was a plus in your favor.

"Man, what's taking them so damn long to let us in?" I asked the question that I'm sure most of them other dudes were thinking. We had been waiting for over thirty minutes in the bitter cold.

"They're fucking with us, dude," Steve said. "I heard one year they made everyone wait for over an hour."

Suddenly, our eyes were drawn to the street, where a slender brother with long braids got out of a baby-blue BMW convertible. I immediately recognized that it was Kevin, a clothes designer who was kind of famous on campus. His designs had premiered in the Homecoming Fashion Show and most women wore his shit on a regular basis. Kevin's popularity was widespread.

No doubt he had mad paper, too, and it was hard to believe someone with his money and fame would even want to join Gamma Phi. Not to put down the frat, but Kevin just didn't fit the profile. He was stylish and feminine—Gamma Phis prided themselves on being ladies' men and masculine. I couldn't see Kevin chillin' with the brothers at parties or getting his ass paddled during the initiation period. Besides, Kevin was openly gay on campus and that was a major strike against him.

"Can you believe this shit, dude?" Steve asked. "I know if this fag gets in, I'm definitely not trying to be down."

I immediately lost respect for Steve. You know, the fact that he was putting down gays. Part of me wanted to punch his ass in the face and let that nigga know what was up with me. But I kept my cool, nonetheless. If I lost it, the attention would turn on me and that wouldn't be good for my image. Man, this shit was nerve-racking, standing out there in the cold and wondering if the other shoe was going to fall at any moment.

I'm now talking about Sheila. I kept looking down the street and wondering if she was going to pull up in the Range Rover. Last time I spoke to Sheila, she was one pissed-off sistah. One word to her cousin Reggie about what went down between us and I was finished on campus. Man, trying to pledge was turning out to be much harder than I realized. I hope Uncle Leonard was right about God seeing me through this though, 'cause a nigga needed all the divine intervention that was out there in the universe to survive the brothers of Gamma Phi Mu.

"Excuse me. You know what time this thing starts?" Kevin picked me out of the crowd. My heart dropped to my ass. Felt like I had to shit. I wondered if he suspected I was down. Sometimes we can spot one another miles away. If it's not in the walk, you can catch that gay fever in the eyes. The eyes are always a dead giveaway. And that's why I avoided Kevin's, staring at the ground instead. "You know what time this thing starts?"

"We been waiting for a while now," I said, being real short and to the point with him. "I suppose it won't be much longer though."

"Thanks." Kevin had a deep, rich voice that didn't go with his feminine look. "I thought I had missed it."

Stop talking to me, dude, I thought to myself. Kevin was bringing more heat my way than a blazing fireplace.

Something about Kevin reminded me of James, who I was trying my damn hardest not to think about today of all days. Maybe that was another reason why I wasn't feeling Kevin being all up in my face. Me and James had fought constantly about me wanting to pledge. He thought I was too old and the whole thing was silly. His inability to support me on all levels, including my desire to be friends with Sheila, only created a rift between us.

Man, I wasn't even speaking with James. Put that nigga out of my apartment when I found out that he had disrespected my pops over this bullshit with Sheila. James showed up at my peeps' house and started going ballistic like some *Fatal Attraction* psychopath. He acted as if me and Sheila were fucking or something. And thanks to him getting up in the woman's face, she didn't even want anything else to do with me. The problem with James was that he took shit too far and blew simple things out of proportion. Now he was going around accusing my family of plotting a conspiracy to get rid of him. If it wasn't for my pops, James wouldn't even be alive, man.

Don't get me wrong. Pops ain't no saint by a long shot. He has spoken against homosexuals on many occasions, and there was a time when Pops wouldn't even speak to me because of my sexuality. But when James was in that hospital fighting for his life, Pops donated his blood without hesitation.

After James got out of the hospital, both my parents made an extra effort to accept him into the family. They invited us to dinners and several family functions, but James couldn't let go of the past. He still felt like my family hated him, especially my brother Carl, who he often called a homophobe. Man, it seemed like things were coming to a head between me and James at the wrong time. But I had to put my needs first, above everything else, including my love for him. It was hard though, 'cause like I said before, I had a lot love for that nigga, man.

"Make sure you have your ID out," said a short dude with round frames who finally opened the doors to the auditorium. His name was Rafer, and I immediately recognized him because Reggie had introduced me to several members of the frat. Most of them knew me by name. "We need to make sure you're registered this semester."

"Here we go," Steve said as we filed in one by one. "It's time to separate the boys from the real men."

"What's up, Johnny?" Rafer dapped me up with a huge smile on his face. "It's good to see you, my man."

"Same here," I said, showing him my ID.

"Where you think you're going?" Rafer immediately stopped Kevin, who was directly behind me, at the door. "Your kind ain't allowed in Gamma Phi."

"And what kind is that?" Kevin asked with an attitude.

"Your kind," Rafer said.

"Is there a problem here?" Reggie joined Rafer at the door. I pretended to be tying my shoe, but the whole time I was observing and listening in on their conversation. When Reggie saw Kevin at the door, he looked shocked, but he kept a professional tone.

"Can we help you with something?" Reggie asked.

"Isn't this a smoker for Gamma Phi Mu?" asked Kevin.

"No, it's not," shouted Rafer behind Reggie's back. "Now get the hell out of here!"

"Hey, bro. No need to act ugly," Reggie said, turning to Rafer. You know, trying to keep the peace. Reggie was simply cool like that—not the type of dude who cared for much drama. He was handsome, too. Reggie was tall, slender, smart, and good-looking with short, sandy brown hair and hazel eyes. Reggie was a damn ten, hands down. Shit, I'll admit it. I even had fantasies about fucking with his fine ass. "This man has every right to show up here like everyone else."

Me and Reggie had become close ever since Sheila introduced us. I looked up to him, man, and that was why I was so afraid of Sheila blasting my business. Although Reggie seemed to be cool with me, there was no telling how he would treat me once he found out that I messed around with dudes.

"Fuck that!" Rafer continued to go ballistic. "Ain't no faggots coming up in our frat!"

Kevin looked hurt. I actually saw tears in his eyes. Of course, I wanted to go to his rescue, man, but defending him would have put me on blast. And I couldn't afford to be outed and risk not making the line. Besides, Kevin was a grown man, and I'm sure this wasn't his first time dealing with hatred. You know, being so openly gay and feminine.

"Forget you bastards," Kevin said as he turned and walked away. "I don't need none of you sorry-ass losers, anyway."

"Good-bye, faggot!" Rafer screamed after him. "And don't show your face around here again!"

"That wasn't called for." Reggie went after Rafer for his behavior. This made me respect him even more. You know, that Reggie would stand up for someone like Kevin. But Reggie was the president of the frat, and he always had the last word. "I'll deal with your ass later."

Man, at that point, I knew this was not going to be an easy process for me. I was trying to be down with a frat that hated "my kind." There was a strong pull in my belly to walk away. I even thought about running out the door with Kevin. But then I thought about Pops, man. He wanted this for me, and I couldn't disappoint him. If I could get through the smoker, then maybe the rest of the process would be much easier. Pops was right. Most of it was a mind game. I had to basically psych myself in order to keep going forward. I had to convince myself that I was pledging for all the right reasons. There are many Rafers out there in the world, but I can't let them stop me. Not now. Not ever.

I took my seat next to Steve and shook off any and all negative thoughts. If I was going to get through this difficult process, I had to be in the right state of mind and keep thinking about that smile on Pops's face. Steve stared in my direction and then patted me on my shoulders.

"You all right, dude?" he asked.

I wiped sweat off my forehead. "I'm cool."

I took in my surroundings. The meeting was inside Rollins Chapel, a medium-size church where they held Sunday-morning service for the student body. The chapel could seat several hundred people comfortably. The windows were huge and decorated with drawings of Jesus, the disciples, and Holy Angels. There were large white columns on both sides of the chapel with red carpet going down the center aisle. It was ironic that Gamma Phi would choose a place of God to hold their smoker.

Wasn't Jesus accepting of all people? Given the scene with Kevin and the frat's overall views on gays, I'm sure Jesus wouldn't approve of their behavior. You know, from everything I've been taught about the Bible—about Jesus' unconditional love. Too bad people don't really practice what they preach. Although we were in the house of the Lord, I'm sure the last thing Rafer was thinking about was the Holy Word. He always put the frat first and everything else second. Rafer was what they called a die-hard member.

"I would just like to make it known," Rafer yelled into the mike. There were about thirty members of the frat standing around him and surveying the audience. They were trying to scope out anyone who was unsuitable from the start. "If you are gay or weak, then this is not the frat for you. I think some other frats on campus, and I won't say their names, are holding their meetings tonight as well."

The brothers laughed. I could feel sweat running down my back. The heater inside that chapel had the entire building hot. Or maybe I was just that uneasy with all this talk about gays.

"We just had to turn one faggot away," Rafer continued, "and we'd be glad to get rid of more of you. I'm sure you've heard about my reputation. Believe it."

"Thank you," Reggie said as he quickly took the mike out of Rafer's hand. "I think everyone gets the point."

There was a rumor on campus that Reggie and several members of Gamma Phi attacked a gay student at a frat party a couple years before I arrived on the scene. The guy was kicked out of the party with severe bruises to his body. Reggie was the one who apparently led the assault on the gay dude, but that was hard to believe given his calm nature and obvious disapproval of Rafer's handling of Kevin. I learned a long time ago not to trust rumors. Sometimes you just gotta get to know somebody for yourself. In my opinion, Reggie could do no harm. He was a real solid brother through and through.

"Now that we got that foolishness out of the way," Reggie said, "let's get down to business."

Reggie spent the next thirty minutes going over the history of the frat and outlining the intake procedures for new members. We were told about the minimum 2.5 grade point average, the community service requirement. At the completion of the process, we would even be given an exam. But most of it was bullshit. Whether or not you had the GPA or did community service, Gamma Phi only took members they *really* wanted and that was the bottom line. You could have a 4.0 GPA, and if they didn't want your ass, then you weren't gonna make the line. I knew it as well as every nigga sitting inside that chapel and hoping to become a member.

"Now join us downstairs in the basement for refreshments," Reggie said with a wide grin on his face. This was when the evening got really interesting.

"Why you wanna be a member of our frat, punk?" One dude held me by the neck while two other members squeezed my arms. Once we got downstairs to the basement, they started roughing us up real bad.

It was crazy, man. They were up in that chapel bitch-slapping niggas and beating their asses as if we were already on line. Gamma Phi was the frat known for serious hazing and had been suspended for going too far at times. The year I tried to pledge was their first year back on the yard in three years.

"Because I believe I can be an asset to the frat?" I said, but it was hard to speak with a nigga's hand around my throat. I looked over to the left of me and saw Steve down on the floor. He had been kicked in the gut by Rafer.

"An asset," I heard one of the members say. He wasn't from Wheatley's chapter, so I didn't recognize him. Sometimes brothers would come from other schools just to beat your ass. This brother was wearing a Howard University T-shirt. "Nigga, you sound like you're interviewing for a commercial."

"Leave him alone, brothers." Reggie walked over and came to my rescue. "Johnny is cool. He's a real brother."

One word from Reggie and those niggas quickly stepped aside and left me alone. Reggie had mad respect, and no one would dare challenge what he had to say. Man, I was just glad to have him on my side, because they were really kicking some ass that night in the chapel. How they were handling us, you would have thought we were being initiated for the Bloods or the Crips. At the end of the day, Gamma Phi was nothing more than a gang of educated brothers.

"Let's take a walk." Reggie patted me on my shoulders and led me upstairs. "You all right, man?"

"I'm good," I lied, trying to be strong. But my body ached from taking punches to my arm and chest. "I can handle whatever."

"That's good to hear," said Reggie, "because this thing ain't for the weak at heart."

Reggie opened the door to the main sanctuary and I followed him down the red carpet. He was heading toward the exit. I noticed he had made a fist. For a minute, I thought he was taking me outside to beat the crap out of me like he did that gay dude on the yard. He must have found out I messed around with dudes. So many crazy thoughts were running through my mind.

"Somebody wanted to holla at you." Reggie must have read the expression on my face. Seen the fear in my eyes. "So relax, nigga. I got your back."

I took in a deep breath and swallowed real hard when Reggie opened the door. Sheila was standing on the outside in a black leather coat. Man, my heart suddenly dropped to my ass. I would have rather taken the beat-down from Reggie instead. At any moment, I was expecting Sheila to put me on blast. Tell Reggie I was gay. And this would have been worse than when my girlfriend from high school, Tonya, told everyone in the hood about my status. At least I could avoid those people by staying home or running out of town. But Wheatley was only so big, and I was bound to run into Reggie or some member of the frat on campus. And I wasn't about to drop out of school over some stupid shit—I had come too far to turn back now.

"What's up, cuz?" Reggie hugged Sheila. "Look at you. All dressed down with the baseball hat and jeans."

"Well, you know, this is how I do it sometimes." She seemed to be in a good mood. "It's good to see you."

"What's up, nigga?" Reggie turned to me. "You're not speaking to my cuz?"

"Of course, man." I went to hug Sheila, but she extended her hand. There was a chill breeze in the air and it wasn't the weather either. "How you been? It's been a minute."

"I've been fine." Sheila had a devilish grin on her face. In that moment, she realized the power in her possession. One word from her about me and James and my ass was toast. My heart was pounding against my chest and my palms were sweaty in fifty-degree weather. "You look nice in your suit and tie."

I was grinning like a cheetah. Reggie placed his arm around my shoulders. "Well, you know I had to get that nigga right. Make sure he represent and come correct."

"You know I try," I joked. Sheila rolled her eyes and I immediately wiped that grin off my face.

"Well, let me leave you two alone for a minute," said Reggie. He kissed Sheila on the cheek. "Good seeing you, cuz. And don't keep my man too long. This his big night."

"Don't worry," Sheila said to Reggie, but her eyes were on me the entire time. "I'm sure this won't take that long at all."

"What's up?" I quickly asked her once Reggie disappeared. "I've been trying to reach you for days. How you been?"

"Why didn't you tell me what was up with you?" Sheila went straight for the jugular. "You led me on. You bastard."

"It wasn't like that." I rushed my words. "You gotta let me explain."

"What is there to explain?" asked Sheila. She was bitter and hurt. Man, her emotions took me by surprise. Me and Sheila had only gone out a few times, and I thought it was on a friendship level. I had no idea she was feeling me like that. "You're gay and you forgot to mention that to me and now your crazy-ass boyfriend has been harassing me at work."

"I'm sorry about that." I swallowed real hard. My whole

body was shaking and my voice was trembling, too. I can't ever recall being that nervous before in my life. "This situation has gotten out of hand."

"You damn right it has!" yelled Sheila. "You give me one good reason why I shouldn't go back in there and tell my cousin everything."

"Look. You do what you gotta do." I suddenly had to man up. If the truth was about to come out, I just had to take my lick. But the last thing I was going to do was let Sheila punk me. At the end of the day, I was still a man. "Like I said, I'm sorry. It wasn't like I tried to mislead you. I thought we were getting to know each other on a friendship level."

"So, you go to the movies and out to dinner and hold hands with all of your friends?" she asked.

"Yeah, sometimes." I had to think about it. "Well, not the holding hands part. But I only did that because you said you were cold and I was trying to keep you warm."

Me and Sheila had gone to the movies to see Tyler Perry's *Diary of a Mad Black Woman*. It was the wrong movie for us to see. Not because it was a bad movie. Man, it was actually great! Tyler is my homeboy, and like every black person I know, I'm crazy about Madea, too, but *Diary* was one of those romantic movies and it put Sheila in a certain mood. After we got out of the movies, she said how cold it was. She was even shivering. Being the gentleman I am, I took her hand, pulled her close to me. That was it: no kissing or fooling around with her. But the moment obviously meant more to Sheila than a simple gesture of goodwill.

"I hear about guys like you." Sheila continued to let me have it. "You have girlfriends and little boyfriends on the side. Well, that shit is sick. And it's wrong! I feel like you were playing games with me and I take that very personal."

"Well, sound like you made up your mind." My patience was running out. Man, I wasn't gonna kiss her or nobody's ass, especially when I knew I was an honest nigga. Sheila had me wrong and that was all there was to it. I can honestly say that I don't take advantage of women for my own pleasure. "But I'm not that type of nigga. I was gone get around to telling you, but that's not just something I tell everybody right away. Would you have hung out with me if I had told you I messed around with dudes? Or introduced me to Reggie and gave me your blessings?"

Sheila stared at me and then rolled her eyes. She folded her arms and thought long and hard about my question. "Probably not."

"My point exactly," I said. "And don't get me wrong. I'm not trying to make excuses, just keeping it real."

"I see." The tension in Sheila's face had softened. She even relaxed her arms. I had put something on her mind. Maybe even hit a nerve.

We suddenly stood there in silence. The chemistry between us was intense. The look in Sheila's eyes was one of a woman strongly desiring a man. What she needed was some dick. I could still read a woman like a book. That's where all that anger was coming from inside her. I stared back at Sheila and wondered if she was willing to go there with me now, knowing my history. Something about the thought of it felt dangerous and exciting.

"Are you two lovebirds finished out here?" Reggie returned and broke the mood.

We both stared at him like teenagers caught with our pants down. She smiled at Reggie, so I figured it was okay for me to smile at him, too.

6

James

"I don't care what you say," said Mookie. He had become my new best friend ever since I was displaced to DC after the hurricane. We met at the Bachclor's Mill over cocktails. Mookie was the one who showed me around DC and schooled me on the game of the streets. Nobody was going to take advantage of me as long as Mookie was in my life. If fact, if it had not been for his friendship and support, I would have completely cracked up when things went south between me and Johnny. "Sounds like that fish after your man, girl."

Me and Mookie were sitting on the sofa in his one-bedroom apartment, listening to some Fantasia on the CD player and getting fucked up. I was drinking Hennessy straight up and Mookie was smoking a joint. The topic of discussion was Johnny and Sheila, of course. You know ain't nothing like having a good friend to get high with when you're going through some really bad shit, honey. Like I said before, Mookie was that friend for me and more.

"And on top of that she messing with your coins, too," Mookie continued to paint a grim picture. "Got you suspended from work. Don't you see she's trying to get rid of you so her and Johnny can be together?"

I took another long pull from the glass, trying to keep myself together, y'all. But it was hard to do because Mookie was right about everything. Ms. Bitch, Sheila, had gotten me laid off from my job for a week without pay. Told Mr. Johnson, the principal, that I was a danger to her as well as those kids. Sheila was cutthroat and she was the real danger to society. It was just that she did a good job masking her true self behind tailored suits and high-heel pumps. So you damn right I was bitter. I loved working with those kids and I needed my money, honey. Period.

Since Katrina, I had been struggling to hold everything together. Had bill collectors calling my ass every time I answered the phone. And FEMA wasn't trying to help a bitch either. I lost all my shit in the flood, and they telling me that I can't get no assistance from the government until an inspector come out and look at my damages.

I'm thinking to myself: Didn't they see the news? I'm from the Ninth Ward and the entire area was destroyed! What fucking more proof did they need? But at the time I couldn't deal with FEMA for thinking about Johnny.

"I can't believe this is happening to me." I shook my head, fighting back tears. "I feel like I'm going through a storm worse than Katrina."

"Okay. Don't go getting all worked up." Mookie patted me on the leg. "I already told you. You can stay with me for a while."

A couple of days ago, I moved into Mookie's apartment when Johnny put me out. You heard me right, honey. Johnny threw my ass out in the cold with no place to go all because I confronted his dad about introducing him to Sheila. And I felt no regrets either, because those people were up to no good. It was so wrong how they were turning Johnny against me. But worse, he couldn't see it.

"I don't wanna believe that Johnny could be with someone else." I took another shot straight down and immediately refilled my glass.

"Well, I got a show tonight," Mookie said, curling his hair. He curled his hair and puffed on a joint at the same time. Mookie did drag on weekends, and it usually took him hours to prepare for one of his shows. "Maybe seeing me perform might cheer you up."

That night he was planning on paying tribute to Whitney Houston, which I knew would go off without a hitch. Nobody could do Whitney better than Mookie, honey. He even resembled Whitney in drag. Mookie was tall and thin—too thin for me—with smooth brown skin just like the real Whitney.

Anyway, I must have sounded like one of Ms. Diva's hit songs, "I Will Always Love You," sitting there drinking my heart out and confessing my undying love for one man. "I will always love Johnny and the thought of him being with someone else hurts too much."

"Girl, take a hit," Mookie said to me, holding the joint in my face. "It'll make you feel a whole lot better."

"No, I'm good," I said. "You know I don't fool with no drugs, honey."

"Well, suit yourself." Mookie took a hit off the joint, blowing smoke in the air. I ain't never met someone who smoked as much weed as Mookie did. Whether morning, noon, or night, Mookie would find some way to work a joint into his daily routine. He smoked so much weed that it was making him lose weight. Like I said before, he was too damn thin for me.

Mookie weighed no more than a hundred pounds, and at first I thought he was sick or something. You know, dying of AIDS. I had lost so many friends to that awful disease that it wasn't even funny. And I didn't want to lose another one. But it wasn't AIDS that was killing Mookie. He claimed to have been tested and the results came back negative. So I figured his skinny ass was taking in too much weed and not enough food. Mookie looked like Whitney Houston on that Michael Jackson special on TV. You know, the one where she looked like a skeleton. That was Mookie and I was worried about him, y'all.

"And you need to stop smoking so much yourself," I said to him, tripping over my words. Honey, I was drunk and could barely talk straight. "'Cause all that weed gone fry your brain one day."

"Bitch, shut up," Mookie said without cutting corners. Although he was real sweet, sometimes Mookie could be so cold and brutal with his words. "You're drunk and in no position to be preaching to me. You need to be worried about that bitch down at that schoolhouse who's about to take your man right from under you."

Out of the blue, I started crying, y'all. Don't know what got into me. Usually, it takes a lot for me to cry, but for some reason I couldn't control my emotions. When Mookie mentioned Sheila taking Johnny away from me, it sent me over the edge. I was bawling like someone had died. And it was some pitiful how I was crying over Johnny, but a man would do it to you, honey. Break you down to nothing and leave your ass broken in pieces.

"Girl, pull yourself together," Mookie said nervously. He had never seen me like this before and really didn't know what else to do for me. I was drunk and beside myself with grief. "Ain't no man worth all of this."

"I think I'm about to throw up," I said. I suddenly jumped off the sofa, ran to the bathroom, and vomited into the toilet bowl. "Oh, God, help me."

The pain in my heart felt like it was smothering me. All I could do was fall to my knees and call on the sweet name of Jesus. You see gays have soul, too, y'all. At that point, nobody but him could make me feel better. He had gotten me through hard times: the death of good friends, Hurricane Katrina, and so much more. Without a doubt, Jesus was my rock, and I never lost sight of that fact throughout this entire mess.

"Please God." I wept across the toilet seat. My whole life revolved around Johnny, and the thought of never seeing him again was too much to bear. "Make everything right between me and Johnny."

"Are you okay, girl?" Mookie watched me from the door. "Do I need to call the people to come get you? You ain't about to kill yourself are you?"

"Just leave me alone!" I shouted at Mookie. "Just leave me alone!"

"I can't do that, sweetie." Mookie picked me up off the floor and led my black ass to the sofa. I was giving more drama than an episode of *The Young and the Restless*. "But you gone be all right, girl. Johnny is madly in love with you. Y'all just going through a tough time. This too shall pass. Trust me."

"You mean that?" I lay down on the sofa, curled up like a newborn. Mookie covered me with a sheet. He took real good care of me.

"Yes, I do." Mookie fluffed my pillow. He looked kind of funny with rollers on one side of his head and the other side real nappy. There was a joint in the corner of his mouth that vibrated like a cell phone. "Maybe we should give your mama a call."

"No!" I shouted in Mookie's face. I knew bringing Flo into this situation would only make matters worse. "Don't do that!"

Don't get me wrong. I love my mama, y'all, but she's straight-up ghetto. You thought I was a drama queen, but Flo took the Oscar from me. That woman think that the only way to handle a problem is with her fist. Flo grew up in the infamous Magnolia Projects in New Orleans, and she had a project mentality at times. One word from Mookie about how Johnny's family had been treating me, and Flo would be in DC on the next plane. And that girl scared to fly, but she would come in a hot minute over someone messing with her son. Flo loved all of her children, honey, even the gay ones. Well, shit, I was the only gay one, but you know what I mean.

"Calm down," Mookie said. "No need to get yourself more upset."

"Just don't call Flo," I cried. "Don't call my mama into this."

"All right, sweetie." Mookie stroked the top of my head to calm me. "I won't call her. Now close your eyes and get some rest. When you wake up, everything will be much better."

"You promise?" I asked, hugging that pillow under my head as if my life depended on it. "You promise?"

As I drifted off to sleep, Mookie went completely silent on me. He never was one to make a lot of promises. When I moved into Mookie's apartment, I had asked him for three months until I got on my feet. Mookie wouldn't commit. He simply said, "Let's take it one day at a time, girl. You know a bitch don't like to make promises she can't keep."

I woke up a half hour later feeling upset and restless all over again. Then I remembered it was Eve's party, and honey, I knew what I had to do.

"I can't believe I let you talk me into this," Mookie said. We were riding in a yellow cab to Johnny's parent's house in Maryland. Mookie was dressed in drag with a ton of makeup on his face. He had on a long black gown and wore high-heel pumps.

As for me, I was wearing a baseball hat and jeans. Not my usual attire. But I wasn't trying to be cute. When you're fighting for your man, honey, sometimes you gotta get down in the gutter.

"I have every right to be there," I said. "I've been a part of that family for over two years."

I had called Johnny to talk about the situation and he hung up in my face without letting me get a word in edgewise. Honey, why did he do that? That was when I came up with the idea to crash the party.

"This is insane," said Mookie. "Those people don't want you there."

"I don't care," I said, holding my forehead. Bitch like me had a headache. My eyes were red and burning like fire. "I'm going anyway."

After about thirty minutes, we pulled up to the house and saw a bunch of expensive cars everywhere. Their guests, like Reverend and Mrs. Lomack, had that paper, honey. We saw nothing but Mercedes-Benzes, BMWs, and Range Rovers on that lawn. You could say that Johnny's parents lived in a mansion, honey, so I expected them to also have friends with cheese. Everyone was at that party, except me and Mookie. But, you know, I was about to put us on the guest list anyway.

"Maybe we should come back later," Mookie said, trying to talk some sense into me, but I wasn't hearing of it.

I ran up a long flight of stairs and rang the door bell. My heart was pumping so fast that my blood pressure must have shot through the roof. We could hear the chatter of folks talking and laughing. There was even soft music playing, but it wasn't hip-hop or rap. This was a bourgeois affair, honey, that turned real ghetto once the door opened and I saw Tiffany's big linebacker-looking ass.

"Oh, bitch, I'm glad you were the one answered the door," I immediately said upon seeing her face. "I've been trying to track you down for a minute."

"This is not the time or place," Tiffany whispered. Although she was dressed in an elegant black gown, that girl looked like a man, honey. Tiffany was tall and big-boned with muscles. You know she was into that bodybuilding bullshit. But big or small, I was ready to take on Ms. Girl for her involvement in breaking up me and Johnny. "You shouldn't even be here."

"Why did you introduce that bitch Sheila to Johnny?" I got right up in her face. Mookie held me by the arm. Must have thought I was gone haul off and slap Tiffany. But it was never my intention to get violent, y'all. I just wanted some answers. That was it. "You get some type of pleasure fucking with my life?"

Tiffany closed the door and stepped out onto the lawn. She obviously didn't want anyone to hear us or see me. They were doing everything in their power to keep me away from Johnny.

"I'm sorry if my actions hurt you," she said, trying to apologize, but I wasn't buying it. That bitch was scared when she saw me and Mookie. Fear was written all across her face. "Let's not allow this to get any more ugly."

"Well, you should have thought about that"–I pointed my finger in her face–"before you and your husband got up in my business."

"Get your motherfucking hands out of my wife's face!" Carl opened the door and got in between me and Tiffany. He immediately set it off on that well-manicured lawn. "You wanna take on somebody. Take it up with me, punk!"

Mookie still had me by the arm, but I quickly pulled away. Got up in Carl's face like we were two football players on the fifty-yard line. He was a big nigga, but I wasn't scared, honey. I had been fighting all my life, and this was just another one for the team. "What you gone do? I've been wanting a piece of your ass from day one. You never did like me and your brother together, anyway!"

"Let's just go," Mookie said, trying to hold me back.

"No, Mookie!" I shouted. "I ain't going nowhere! I'm tired of these people fucking with me!"

"You better listen to your friend . . ." Carl said, pointing his finger in my face. We both were pointing at each other. And while Mookie tried to contain me, Tiffany had Carl by one of his arms, too. ". . . before you get your punk ass beat down out here."

"Fuck you!" I said. "Fuck you and your man-looking-ass wife!"

Then, bam. Carl punched the shit out of me. He punched me so hard I fell on my ass on the ground. For a moment, the whole world seemed to be spinning.

"Oh, no, you didn't punch my friend," Mookie said, reaching inside his bra. Mookie always kept a switchblade inside that bra of his. Most queens carried a knife for protection from ignorant, ass-straight dudes who often threaten them for dressing up like women. I had actually seen Mookie cut a man across his face for shouting insults at him.

"Show me how bad you are now." Mookie waved the blade in front of Carl's face while I sat on the ground and tried to regain my composure.

"What the hell is going on out here?" Johnny ran down the stairs and immediately took control of the situation. If he had not showed up, I don't even wanna think about what would have happened. "Mookie, put that knife away."

"These fags have lost their minds," Carl said, "coming on this property and disturbing the peace."

"That didn't give you no right to hit me," I replied. I finally was able to stand up. My mouth felt numb and bruised. I could taste the blood from a broken tooth.

"First of all, what are you doing here?" Johnny looked me right in the eyes and spoke to me like a stranger. That's what hurt the most: the look in his eyes and the sound of his voice like he didn't love me anymore. "Why you keep causing trouble? I'm getting sick of this shit, man."

"So you're saying this my fault?" I asked, holding my lip. It was busted. "You know how much your brother hates me. Can't you see they're trying to break us up?"

"And can't you see," Carl said, "that my brother doesn't want anything else to do with your punk ass?"

Me and Carl have never gotten along, honey. While most of Johnny's family had accepted me, Carl always showed his disapproval. On Thanksgiving last year, he showed up at the family dinner and made a scene. Told everyone that he wasn't eating at no table with no punk-ass nigga. Johnny and him fought. Back then, Johnny was always defending me.

"Let's just go, girl." Mookie grabbed me by the arm. "They ain't even worth our time."

I stood there and stared Johnny directly in the face. There was a small part of me hoping that he would ask me to stay. Tears even welled up in the corner of my eyes. You know me and Johnny had so much history, and nothing about this situation was easy.

"You should go," Johnny said, "before my family figure out what's going on out here and call the police."

Mookie had pulled out his cell phone and called someone while me and Johnny went back and forth. Tiffany and Carl stood behind Johnny as if he needed backup from me. It was a crying shame how they were treating me as if I was suddenly public enemy number one.

"I don't care about the police," I said with tears falling from my eyes. Why couldn't Johnny see how much I loved him? How much he was hurting me? "I love you and I wanna make things right."

"You can't make things right," he told me. Johnny was so cold that I didn't even recognize him. "Too much has happened."

"We been through worse," I said, "and we can get through this."

"We have to get back to the party," Carl said, interrupting us. "I'm sure Grandma probably looking for us."

"Just leave us alone!" I shouted. "This has nothing to do with you!"

"He's right. I have to go," Johnny said to me. It felt like he was choosing Carl over me and that made the pain stick like glue. This wasn't like Thanksgiving when Johnny was completely on my side. "Be cool. I'll call you later. I promise."

"Well, go ahead," I said to Johnny as he followed Carl and Tiffany inside the house. "You're partying in a big mansion with your family and hanging out with college kids. So you don't need me now, huh? Well, fuck you, Johnny!"

Johnny slammed the door and never once looked back at me. He had definitely changed, and I had no idea what was going on with him. How can you be in love with someone one day and the next day find them completely unrecognizable? Like you had been sleeping with a stranger the entire time. Needless to say, I wept uncontrollably inside of Mookie's arms.

"It's gone be all right, sweetie," Mookie said, rubbing my back.

Suddenly, one of Mookie's friends pulled up in a baby-blue BMW. He had money, too, and lived in the area.

"This is my friend Kevin," Mookie said to introduce us. Kevin was slender with braids and kind of cute, too. "And, Kevin, this is James."

"Nice to meet you." Kevin had a deep voice. "Sorry about what you're going through."

I stared at Mookie as he climbed into the backseat. He had such a big mouth for calling someone else into a very private matter.

"I had to tell him something," explained Mookie. He knew I was not feeling his friend being all up in my business.

"Sorry. Did I say or do something wrong?" asked Kevin. I could sense that he was a really nice guy.

"No, you good," I lied, locking my seat belt in place. I stared out of the window. Johnny was standing in the doorway, watching us. Maybe he still cared; at least that's what a part of me was hoping.

I stared at Kevin. "Kiss me."

"Excuse me?" he asked.

"Damn bitch you do move fast," Mookie joked.

With Johnny standing in the door, I only had a small window of opportunity. Therefore, I couldn't wait for Kevin to make a move, honey. I leaned over that seat and landed his ass with a kiss that I'm sure Johnny would not soon forget.

7

Sheila

"Sweetheart, maybe you should move back home," my mom said to me for the zillionth time. She thought my life was pretty much pitiful. Here I was, alone, divorced with no kids, and turning thirty in a couple of months. In Mom's eyes, it just wasn't normal for a woman to be without a man and kids at my age. She had married Dad in her early twenties. "Most of your family is here in New Orleans."

"I'm not moving back to that god-awful city, Mom," I said to her, sitting on the sofa, polishing my nails and trying to get geeked up to attend a fund-raiser for students in the DC public schools. My simpleminded boss, Diane, had insisted that I make an appearance on behalf of Advantage Principles. She said there would be music and food and free cocktails. On the surface, it sounded like a nice affair, but being around a bunch of stuffy executives talking about politics and education the entire night was not my idea of a good time.

"Hell, I don't know why you and Dad insist on being there, anyway," I continued with Mom. "Things have just gotten worse since Katrina."

Please don't misunderstand me. I love my fair city of New Orleans, but we had some major issues long before Katrina. I have to be totally honest about this thing. The education system was a joke and the crime rate was shamefully high. Homicides were a daily headliner, and the economy was on a steady decline with no relief in sight. And it looked like everywhere you turned people were suffering, even in my own family. Moreover, I had seen poverty and decay strike down the lives of decent and hardworking citizens in that city. And to be honest, it was very depressing.

Of course, we have our attractions like Mardi Gras, jazz, and great food. However, that's only part of the story. Most people don't get to see other sections of New Orleans where the common folk live. Where single mothers struggle every day to keep food on the table and try to raise kids without their fathers in a less-than-ideal set of circumstances. And for those reasons alone I left the city after high school with no intention of ever returning. Katrina only sealed the deal for me.

"Things are getting better," Mom insisted. She and Dad were among the first residents to move back after the storm. Although I had tried to get them to stay in DC with me, they had refused. Mom and Dad had lived in that city their entire lives and knew of nothing else. At their age, they weren't going to try to start over in an unfamiliar place. "Folks are returning and rebuilding. I do worry about Marshall though. Since most of the staff haven't returned to the hospital, he's working so hard."

Hell, I should have known it was coming. Before long, I knew Mom would play the sympathy card and try to get at my emotions. Although she's a strong woman by nature, Mom could come across as weak and pathetic. She loved being the victim, a trait I definitely avoided at all cost.

"He's been complaining about having headaches," Mom continued. "He just won't slow down, sweetheart. And my pressure done gone up. Doctor got me on medication."

I laid the phone down on the sofa and placed Mom on speaker, so my nails could air dry. She was working my last good nerve. "Why didn't you tell me about all of this before, Mom?"

"You have me on speaker, sweetheart?" she asked. "You know how much I hate being on speaker."

I picked up the phone, removed the speaker command. "Now why didn't you tell me, Mom?"

"Because we don't like to worry you, sweetheart," she said, "but we gone be all right down here. Don't you worry about us. You got enough to deal with up there."

"Well, I do worry," I said, now polishing my toes and thinking about what dress I should wear and with what pumps. There was a sexy black dress that came just above the knees that had been hanging in my closet for weeks and calling my name. "So don't keep things from me. I'm a big girl, Mom. I can handle it."

"I know, sweetheart," she said. "Anyway, let's talk about something else. Are you still seeing that young man you were telling me about? The one who's attending Wheatley?"

"Nope," I said with a bitter taste in my mouth. "Things didn't work out for us."

"I'm sorry, sweetheart," Mom said. "You seemed to really like him. What happened?"

"Let's just say," I said, "I wasn't Johnny's type."

One mention of Johnny's name and my stomach began to churn. That man got to me more than I cared to admit. The truth was, I wanted to hate him, but I couldn't. I had even gone so far as going up to Wheatley with the intention of exposing Johnny to my cousin Reggie. Gamma Phi was having their annual smoker, and I knew Johnny would be in attendance.

I know a lot of brothers of Gamma Phi, and they are not too keen on gay men joining their frat. And Reggie would be hurt. He really took a strong liking to Johnny. I've never known Reggie to hate gays, but I know for certain he doesn't choose to hang out with any of them either. Bottom line, my presence would be bad for Johnny all the way around, so I was very careful about not letting my emotions get the best of me.

Besides, after speaking with my therapist, I had learned to take some responsibility for my own actions. Johnny was not completely to blame for me getting the wrong idea about our relationship. He had only asked me out as a friend, and I had taken his kindness to mean more than friendship. Johnny was definitely a departure from what I was used to in terms of dealing with the opposite sex. Most men I had dated in the past were trying to get in the panties. Hell, I can't be any more real than that.

"Maybe you should get out more instead of always working," Mom said, pushing her agenda. "I'm sure there are lots of available men out there to date."

Mom was the type who believed that a woman couldn't be happy unless there was a man in her life. Maybe that explained why she had forgiven Dad for so many of his indiscretions, because she feared being alone. And the fact that there had not been a steady man in my life in quite a while was what had Mom so worried about me. In her sight, this constituted a major crisis.

"I'm actually getting out and attending a fund-raiser tonight," I told her, hoping to put her fears to rest. "So maybe I'll get lucky and meet a nice, fine millionaire who'll sweep me off my feet. Then I won't have to work so hard."

"You're going out alone?" Mom actually sounded sorry for me—one of the reasons I didn't want to tell her in the first place. Although Mom had good intentions, she had a way of making me feel like something was wrong with me. You know, the fact that I didn't have a man in my life to call my own. "Sweetheart, you couldn't find an escort?"

"Mom. I love you." I said to her. She knew she was pushing it, but that didn't stop her in the least bit.

"You shouldn't be going out to an event alone," Mom said. "That would make you look very desperate."

I ignored her, laid the black dress across the bed, and imagined myself working the room in it. Entering the fund-raiser with that dress on would be worth the trip whether I met a man or not. But every dress needed the proper accessories. I couldn't decide between the diamond earrings or the simple hoop ones I bought from a corner vendor. The diamond earrings were an anniversary gift from Ken a few years ago. If nothing else, that bastard did have good taste. However, I decided to go for simplicity instead of being ostentatious.

"Sweetheart, are you still there?" asked Mom.

"Yeah, Mom, but I do have to go," I said, rushing her off the phone. "I'll call you tomorrow."

"But sweetheart—"

"Bye, Mom," I said. "Give Dad my love."

When I entered the ballroom, I was blown away by the décor. The place was decorated with flowers and balloons. The room was dimly lit, with hundreds of tables that looked as though the china could have been placed by Martha Stewart herself. Everything was just so perfect and elegant. The crowd was a mix of educators, business executives, politicians, and students from the various high schools, and they all looked exquisite. Waiters paraded around, serving light finger food and wine. Of course, there was soda and water for the kids. I quickly grabbed a glass of white wine to calm my nerves.

"Sheila, you made it." Diane glided up and greeted me with a kiss on both cheeks. She was wearing a long black gown and looking quite stunning. Diane lived for these type of affairs, where she could boast about Advantage Principles' success

rate with public schools and how she was responsible for helping low-income black kids from the hood. It made me sick to
the stomach. Most of that success was due to my hard work,
but Diane took the credit. Here she worked out of her office in
Baltimore while I traipsed through the hood making Advantage Principles look good.

"I like this dress, girl," I said to her, making polite conversation. Hell, she was still my boss. I wasn't that crazy. "And you're
working those pumps."

"You're looking good, too," she said. "Maybe you'll find Mr.
Right tonight."

Diane knew all about my recent relationship drama with
Johnny because most of my personal business had been floating around the schools. It was daily gossip for the lunchroom,
thanks to James and some of the nosey-ass teachers who
couldn't keep their mouths closed. It was horrible how both
James and Johnny seemed to be dominating every aspect of
my life lately. Actually, it had become annoying and embarrassing for me, and I honestly didn't know how much more of
it I could take.

"Maybe I will," I said graciously, "but until then I think I'll
have another cocktail."

I stopped a handsome young waiter who couldn't keep his
eyes off me. The black dress was working and turning heads.

"Thank you," I said as I smiled at him, placed the empty
glass on the tray, and grabbed another glass of wine. Diane
stared at me real hard.

"Not too many of those now," she said. "I need you in your

mind tonight. There are some important people here who I'm hoping will make generous donations to our program."

I look a long gulp from the glass and caught my breath. "Okay. I'm with you. Let's work the room."

Diane introduced me to everyone, from the chairman of the *Washington Post* to the mayor of DC. There were so many important people in that room that it was hard to keep track. I was very proud to see that there was a special night dedicated to raising money for our kids. It was such a worthy cause. And, personally, I've always been of the belief that investing in a child is really preparing for our future. We will need them to make new discoveries about how to live more peacefully and healthfully on this great planet of ours.

"Sheila, is that you?" I heard a voice floating across the room. It was none other than my best friends who betrayed me. I'm talking about Tiffany and Carl. Seeing them at the fund-raiser changed my whole mood. "I had no idea you would be here."

"Excuse me, Sheila," Diane said. She made eye contact with someone across the room. And I was sorry that she did. The last thing I wanted was to run into Carl and Tiffany. They weren't my favorite people in the world those days.

"I think I see a former colleague of mine," continued Diane. "You'll be okay."

"Go ahead." I managed a smile. "I'm a big girl. I'll meet up with you later."

"Hey, girl." Tiffany walked over with Carl on her arm. They were grinning as if everything was good between us. "It's such a surprise seeing you here."

"I have nothing to say to either one of you." I was cold and bitter with them. "I'm still very upset."

"Come on now, Sheila," Carl said. He was wearing a black tuxedo and looking completely out of his element. Carl was the jock type who lived for ESPN. "How long this shit gone go on? Don't you think you're taking this a bit too far?"

I took another sip from the glass; my head was suddenly spinning. "You really don't want to go there with me. Because you and your brother are quite a piece of work."

"How much have you had to drink?" asked Tiffany. "You sound like you've already had too much."

"I'm fine." I gritted the words between my teeth. "Until I saw the two of you. What are you doing here, anyway?"

Tiffany fixed Carl's crooked tie. She worshipped the ground that man walked on. "Carl just got a major executive position with the school board."

I raised my glass in the air. "Good for you. Maybe the job will keep you busy, so you won't have time to stick your nose in my business."

"For what it's worth," he said, "my brother really likes you."

"I hate to break it to you, Carl," I said, "but your brother is gay. So deal with it."

The look on his face was priceless. It was sad, but Carl was in such denial regarding Johnny's sexuality. He tried to maintain a smile on his face, but the hurt was evident.

"That's real cold," he said. "You didn't even have to go there."

"I'm just stating the facts," I responded. "He's a homo, so get over it."

"Man, you better chill with all that." His entire face had turned demonic. At this point, I was really getting to Carl, and that was my intention. As far as I was concerned, he deserved it. What they both did—introducing me to Johnny without letting me know the deal with him—was dead wrong. There was no other way to cut it. I didn't deserve being bamboozled. "That's still my brother you're talking about."

"Okay, you guys, that's enough." Tiffany stood in between us. "Carl, could you give me and Sheila a moment alone?"

"Gladly," Carl said as he grabbed a glass of wine from the handsome waiter and disappeared into the crowd. The music was starting to get much better and people were even dancing. They must have switched DJs or something, because this party was suddenly coming alive and happening.

"You know that wasn't called for," said Tiffany. I flagged down a waiter and grabbed another glass of wine, snapping my fingers to the music. "And you need to slow your roll."

"You ain't my mama," I said, sipping from my glass. "And I'm still mad at you."

"Oh, my God!" Tiffany exclaimed. The girl was looking as if she had suddenly seen Jesus Christ or something. Her eyes were wide; her mouth was open.

"What's wrong with you?" I asked.

"Don't look," she said, "but Ken just walked in the door."

I turned around and made direct eye contact with him. "Oh, damn."

"I told you not to look," said Tiffany.

"What is he doing here?" I wondered out loud. "I hope he didn't see the reaction on my face. I don't need this tonight."

"Brace yourself," said Tiffany. "He's walking toward us. Ken, how are you?"

"I thought that was the two of you," Ken said.

I turned to face him with a tight grin on my face. The last time I had seen him was in the courtroom at our divorce a few years prior. It is unbelievable how time flies.

Why did he have to be looking so good, I thought to myself. Ken was tall and handsome. He had broad shoulders and a huge, manly chest. The round frames and short Afro gave him a retro seventies look.

"This is definitely a pleasant surprise," said Ken.

"Same here," Tiffany said. I remained silent while the two of them played catch-up. "What you been up to, Ken? God, how many years has it been?"

"It's been a long time." He smiled, staring at me real hard. His smile had seduced me many times. I look a sip from my glass. "I'm running my own real estate company. You know the market is hot now."

"That's really great," Tiffany said. "I'm happy for you."

"And what about you?" asked Ken. "You're looking quite fit. Almost didn't recognize you, girl."

"Thank you," Tiffany said. "I'm bodybuilding and competing every chance I get."

"That's cool." He was smiling at me once again. I took another pull from my glass. My knees felt weak. And I could feel a run in my stockings. You know the run always happens at the most inconvenient time. "You're pretty quiet."

"Who, me?" I said daintily, trying to maintain my composure.

"Is there someone else here?" asked Ken with a bit of an attitude that quickly reminded me of what a first-rate jerk he was. He was just as arrogant and cocky as ever. "You're standing here like the cat got your tongue or something."

"I'm tired," I said tartly. "Is that okay with you?"

Tiffany nudged me in the back. She wanted everyone to play nice and keep the peace.

"Well, maybe you should have stayed home," he said. "Got you some rest. You're not looking as fresh as you used to."

"What do you want, Ken?" I was tired of making small talk with him. There was nothing friendly between us. We had a messy, ugly divorce. If I never saw him again in my life, it would have been fine with me. "And why are you even here? 'Cause you're too selfish to give a damn about these kids."

"I'm hurt," he said. Suddenly, a beautiful, short, light-skinned woman joined us. I noticed she was pregnant. Her face looked familiar.

"There you are, honey," she said as she grabbed Ken by the arm and gave me and Tiffany the once-over. She was acting like an insecure woman in a room full of beautiful women. You should have seen her grabbing and pulling on Ken's arms. Why do we always have to be in competition when it comes to men? "I've been looking all over for you."

"Sorry to worry you, baby." He kissed her. Something about

Ken was different. He seemed more affectionate with this woman than he had ever been with me. "I ran into some old friends."

"Nice to meet you," she said, extending her hand. "My name is Jackie."

"I know you," Tiffany said. "You're the new weather lady."

"Yes, that's me," she said. "I just started a month ago. And would you say I've been pretty accurate with the weather?"

"You've been on point." Tiffany made nice with her, but I suddenly needed something stronger than wine.

"Thank you," she said. "I try."

"You do more than try, baby." Ken kissed her in front of me again. I think that bastard was deliberately trying to get to me. And it was working big time. "Jackie and I are expecting our first child."

Tiffany squeezed my hand. She must have sensed how hard this was for me. The problems and issues between us faded in comparison to this situation. No one knew better than Tiffany how difficult it was for me to move on after Ken.

"She's giving me something no woman ever could," Ken said and stared me in the face. You should have seen the grin on his face. He was definitely being cruel.

"You bastard." I tossed what was left of that wine in his face and ran off.

"Sheila, wait up!" Tiffany caught up with me in the parking lot. "Don't worry about him. He's an asshole."

"Hey, I'm good," I lied, trying to maintain my balance. The ground felt like it was moving. "Never felt better."

"You don't have to put up a front for me," said Tiffany. "He was a jerk for throwing that baby in your face."

The first year of our marriage, Ken and I got pregnant. I miscarried and was told that I would never be able to carry a baby to term. There was something wrong with my uterus. Instead of being the supportive husband, Ken often criticized me for not being able to carry children like a normal woman. In fact, he threw the situation in my face all the time, which made me quite insecure in our marriage.

I stood out on the street and tried hailing a cab. "Where's a cab when you need one?"

"Why don't you let me and Carl take you home?" suggested Tiffany. She was being so supportive and nice to me.

"I'd rather take a cab." I was cold and bitter. "But thanks for asking. Now go back inside and enjoy yourself. I'm okay. Really."

I don't remember much else about that night. All I know was that the sun was burning my eyes and peeping through my blinds the next morning. My entire body felt bruised, like I had had a fierce workout at the gym with Tiffany. She was known for pushing things to the limit. Anyway, I had the worst headache in the world, too. And I was naked. Hell, I didn't even remember taking off my clothes. Usually, I slept in my cute white pajamas with the little yellow ducks. Why was I naked?

I suddenly heard the toilet flushing and I realized that I was not alone. My heart started racing. There was a stranger in my house. I immediately picked up the phone to dial 911.

"What's up, baby? I see you finally got up, huh?"

I dropped the phone on the floor. "Johnny, what the hell are you doing in my house?"

8

Johnny

"Rape." Mr. Poindexter's lecture on the rape epidemic on college campuses sent chills running through my entire body. He was my Intro to Law professor, and the class was one of my favorites at Wheatley. Usually, I would be all in dude's mouth, hanging on every word, but for some reason I couldn't stay focused on his lesson for nothing in the world. It was like the shit he was saying was really getting under my skin and making me nervous. "Happens to one in four college women. Most of them say they were attacked by someone they knew."

I suddenly grabbed my backpack and ran out of the classroom. I ran and parked my ass on a nearby bench on the main yard. My hands were literally shaking and I felt like I had loose bowels or something. Not much action was happening on the yard either, 'cause it was freezing and you know black folks don't like being out in the cold. Besides a few people trying to

make it to class, it was just me, the loose bowels, and two squirrels that were running and playing around my feet.

They suddenly ran past me and up a tree. I figured the squirrel doing the chasing was probably the male squirrel. I wanted
to tell him to run in the other fucking direction. A lil' piece of
ass ain't worth the headache in the long run. Believe me. I
know. The other night me and Sheila fucked around and now
you wouldn't believe what that bitch was accusing me of. It
was insane, man—some serious and twisted propaganda.

I had been really worried about Sheila. You know, after she
found out about me and James. When she showed up at the
smoker, I could tell she was really hurt, man. And one thing
about me: I don't like to see anyone in pain, especially a beautiful woman. Only thing I wanted to do was make things right.
So I tried calling her a couple of times, but she wasn't answering my calls. Part of me was worried about her, but honestly I
wanted to know what type of shit she was on. You know, why
she really showed up at the smoker in the first place. To be
truthful, I thought she was going to march up in there and tell
her cousin Reggie everything. But she didn't.

Of course, I was grateful to her, man. I don't even want to
think about what would have happened had she told them
dudes in the frat what was really up with me. Still, I couldn't
figure Sheila out. Why was she even protecting me? Maybe it
was a game and she was planning on setting me up at another
time. I had so many twisted thoughts running through my
mind that I had to get the situation cleared up once and for all.

After several unreturned calls, I showed up at Sheila's door. I knocked and rang her doorbell so many times, I figured she wasn't home or in a deep sleep. It was late, but I wasn't caring about the time. When I got something heavy on my mind, I have to get to the bottom of it one way or the other. Needless to say, I was just about to give up on talking to Sheila that night when she answered the door. Man, she came to the door in her bra and panties. That took a nigga completely by surprise. The bra and panties definitely set the mood for the rest of the night.

"Don't you know how late it is?" she asked. Her words seemed slurred, and I could tell she had been crying. Her eyelashes were stuck to her skin and mascara was running down her face. It wasn't hard for me to figure out that Sheila was drunk, too. "And I'm tired. Not a good time for company."

"What's wrong with you?" I followed her inside the apartment. *She let me in.* She let me in and laid across the sofa. I noticed she had a bottle of vodka on the table in front of her. It was empty. "Talk to me."

"Nothing's wrong." She held her forehead. "Can't a girl just be tired if she wants to?"

I tried not to stare at her titties, but they were right up in my damn face. I couldn't miss them if I wanted to. Sheila's titties looked like juicy, ripe watermelons, and her legs were nicely shaped and toned. I had always imagined what she would look like with her clothes off. Man, Sheila had a tight-ass body and was sexy as hell! But I wasn't even trying to go there with her. I don't care how sexy she was. I'm not the type of dude who takes advantage of vulnerable women. The last thing Sheila needed was my dick inside of her. That woman needed someone to talk to and that was my intention from the beginning. Nothing more and nothing less, but Sheila had other ideas... Not me.

"How much you had to drink?" I picked up the bottle and held it in front of her.

She rolled over on the sofa with her ass sunny-side up. She had on a sexy pair of tight red panties. Her butt cheeks were showing. She took a long stretch, flexing her butt muscles in my face. "Why you worrying about it? What are you doing here anyway?"

"I wanted to talk to you." I placed the bottle back on the table, trying not to stare at Sheila's fat ass. My dick was hard, but I kept a straight face. I was in control of my dick, not the other way around. "I've been worried about you."

"That's your problem." She turned to face me. She had a maniacal look in her eyes like I had never seen before. Maybe it was the running mascara, but Sheila wasn't looking like herself. "You talk too much," she said.

Sheila reached over and grabbed my dick inside my pants. I swear, man. She grabbed my dick and started stroking it.

"What are you doing?" I didn't know what else to say. Although her hand on my dick was feeling real good, something about it wasn't right. Sheila was drunk and I couldn't take advantage of her. On the surface, I knew that shit wasn't right. I should have stopped her, but I didn't. I couldn't. The beast inside of me was too strong.

"What you think I'm doing?" She placed a finger in her mouth, trying to seduce me. "You scared of me or something?"

"Scared?" I quickly started to man up. Sheila probably already thought I was weak or less of a man after finding out about me and James. It still mattered to me how women viewed me. "I ain't scared of nothin'."

"Damn." She placed a finger inside her panties. "I'm feeling so nasty."

"That's the alcohol talking," I said to her. "You've had too much to drink. Let me make you some coffee."

I stood up to leave, but she grabbed hold my hand. There was a maniac look in her eyes again. "Don't leave me."

"I'm just going in the kitchen," I said. "I'm coming right back."

"Just hold me," begged Sheila. She pulled me down to the sofa and wrapped her arms around my neck. She was squeezing me tight and weeping like someone who had lost a close friend or relative. "Just hold me and never let go."

"What's wrong?" I asked her again. The way Sheila was holding me and crying on my shoulder really had me worried. Man, you don't understand. This was a strong, well-put-together woman, and I had never seen her like this before. Somebody had broken her down, and I knew this had nothing to do with me or the situation with James. "Somebody did something to you?"

"He knew I couldn't have children," Sheila cried. But the more she tried to explain herself, the more confused I became. "And he had to throw that bitch in my face."

"Who are you talking about?"

"I don't wanna talk about it." Then she started kissing me out of the blue. She was kissing me and was all on top of a nigga that I could hardly catch my breath. "Make love to me."

"I don't think that's a good idea," I said, although my dick was poking against my jeans. "You've been drinking."

"I'm a big girl. I know what I'm doing." She started unzipping my pants. There was a big voice inside my head telling me to stop her. But there was another horny, freaky voice saying, "Go for it." So I did.

Sheila took my dick out of my pants and started sucking me off. And it was on and popping from there. Once I was in the zone there was no turning back. I held my head back, biting my top lip. Sheila was sucking the hell out of my dick, so that even my toes were on hard. Her sexy lips felt so moist and wet that I wanted to scream, but I kept biting my lip instead.

"Damn, this dick taste good." She started rubbing my chest while sucking my dick at the same time. I rubbed the top of her head and placed my hand on her fat ass. "Damn. I wanna feel this dick inside of me."

She suddenly stopped sucking me off and told me to stand up. She was leading and I was following her every command. Man, I couldn't believe this shit was even happening, let alone how freaky Sheila was acting. She made me realize what I had been missing not being with women. Once me and James started kicking it, I had decided not to be with anyone else— not even a woman. But that night I wanted to come inside some wet pussy. I ain't gone lie about that either. I had missed that feeling. Don't get me wrong. A piece of boy ass is good, but there was still nothing like diving inside of some warm pussy.

"Don't be afraid." She took off her bra and placed my hand on her titties. "They don't bite."

"Oh, believe me," I said, squeezing her titties and smiling like a kid in a candy store, "I don't mind if they do."

She took off my shirt and started biting at my neck. I don't remember how I got out of my pants or drawers, because shit was happening so fast. One minute we were standing up, kissing and sucking. And the next thing I was sitting on the sofa naked and Sheila was riding my dick like a cowboy. But with all the excitement I was still trying to be responsible. Man, I was inside of her raw and knew that wasn't cool.

"Wait," I said. "I don't have on a condom."

"Just pull out," she said, bouncing up and down on top of my dick. And it was feeling too good to have her stop. She was giving me that pussy raw and uncut, like we were two animals out in the wild. Man, it was crazy. Me and Sheila were fucking like two lions out in the jungle. And if it was wrong, a nigga for damn sure didn't wanna be right that night. So I kept hitting her raw and forgot all about the condom.

"Damn, this feels good," said Sheila while riding my dick. She got up off of me and leaned across the sofa. She wanted me to hit her from the back, doggy style. I stood up behind her, and she grabbed my dick and pushed it in. She started throwing her ass back.

"Grab my hair." Sheila wanted to play wild, so I snatched a handful of her hair. I grabbed her hair and started thrusting my ass harder and harder. She was screaming and moaning, so I knew a nigga was doing his job right. That shit made me feel good, too. Having my dick inside of Sheila and hearing her scream my name made me feel like King Kong on top of the Empire State Building. The only thing that was left to do was beat my chest, but I tried to break my dick off inside of her instead.

"Fuck. This pussy wet," I said, smacking her sexy black ass. Sheila was darker than chocolate, and they always say the blacker the berry, the sweeter the juice. It felt like my dick was about to explode inside of her. "Throw that ass back."

"Wait. I want it another way." She jumped on top of me and wrapped her legs around my waist. I started grabbing her ass and fucking her standing up. I was fucking and walking her lil' ass all over the house. We were knocking over furniture and tearing at each other like savage beasts. Her titties tasted like honey, maple syrup. And don't even ask me how we ended up in the bedroom either. But somehow we did.

"I'm about to come!" she was screaming with her legs wrapped around my waist.

"Fuck!" I yelled. "Me, too!"

And we both did. We got our nut and fell on top of the bed. Both of us were breathing like our asses had run an African marathon or something. And you know them lil' motherfuckers in Africa can run far.

"You wore my ass out," I said to her. "I need to get back in the gym."

When I looked over, Sheila was passed out beside me. She

was passed out and snoring her ass off. It was cute though. She looked so innocent and pretty while sleeping. Whatever was worrying Sheila when I arrived earlier that night didn't seem to be bothering her anymore. I kissed her on the forehead and curled up next to her. You know I didn't want Sheila to wake up and find me gone. Think I was some hit-and-run type of nigga. I had mad respect for Sheila and I wasn't trying to make her feel like no whore.

The following morning I came out of the shower, dick swinging and hoping for a repeat of last night. But when Sheila saw me, she started talking crazy. She claimed that she couldn't remember a single thing about what had happened. She pulled the too-drunk-to-remember routine. Man, that bitch was on some other shit for real, throwing the big "R" word around in the air like I forced myself on her or something.

And that was why my ass was now sitting on the yard in the bitter cold with a long face, thinking about my fate and watching two squirrels fucking. This was not what I imagined my college experience would be like. It was supposed to be simple. Go to class, make good grades, party hard, and fuck without consequences. Now my ass was looking at rape charges if Sheila followed through with her threats.

You damn right I was scared, man. The idea of going back to the pen was a terrifying idea. Being locked down and caged like an animal was like slavery all over again. I couldn't go through that shit again. I would kill myself before going back to the pen.

"What's up, Johnny?" A voice snuck up from behind and

interrupted my thoughts. I turned around and saw that it was Kevin. You know, the gay dude who was turned away from the smoker. I was hoping to avoid this moment, but I knew it was coming anyway.

"I gotta go to class," I said. I clutched my backpack and immediately stood up. "I'll holla at you later."

"That's wrong how you're treating him," Kevin said. I looked around to see if anyone was watching us. The last thing I needed was for Reggie or other frat members to see us together. After the incident with Sheila, a nigga didn't need any more heat. "That boy loves you."

The other night, James showed up at my peeps' place. Man, he showed up with his drag-queen friend Mookie, and they were trying to crash my grandma's eightieth birthday. I came outside and he was trying to fight my brother Carl, too. And you know that shit wasn't right, man. Regardless of what was going on between me and him, my family didn't have anything to do with our mess, contrary to what James thought. I was the one who decided to put an end to our relationship—not my family.

"Look, dude," I said, looking over my shoulder to see if anyone was around. My ass was so fidgety and nervous that it didn't even make any sense. "I appreciate your concern, but this has nothing to do with you."

"I was just letting you know that boy is hurting," Kevin said, tossing his scarf over his shoulders. He had on a long, expensive trench coat and a trendy plaid hat that matched perfectly with the scarf. No matter what they said negative about Kevin on campus, they couldn't knock his fashion sense. Dude always looked like he just stepped off a cover of *GQ* magazine or something. "And what you saw the other night was not what it seemed."

"Whatever, man," I said to him with a smirk on my face. After I forced James to leave the party, Kevin came pulling up in front of the house in his BMW. Of course, I was blown away by seeing Kevin. I had no idea he and James even knew one another, let alone were close enough to be kissing. You heard me right, man. James got inside of Kevin's BMW and started kissing the dude. It wasn't like I was jealous or anything, but just telling what happened. "I know what I saw."

"He kissed me to try and make you jealous," Kevin said. "But it was nothing. All I'm saying if you want him back, you can get him."

Two females from my English class suddenly glided by us and smiled. They were sorority girls. I wondered what they were thinking. You know, seeing me on the yard talking with Kevin. One of them was a tall, skinny girl with long black hair. I had seen her kicking it with Reggie at a basketball game. Reggie had a lot of women, so she could be one of his whores. That's what Reggie called his women on campus.

"Earth to Johnny." Kevin waved his hand in my face. I had gotten so caught up on the two females that I lost my train of thought. "Are you hearing a word I'm saying to you?"

"How do you know James, anyway?" I got straight to the point with him.

"Me and him both friends with Mookie," Kevin said. "He

and I have been friends for as long as I can remember. That's where James is staying if you care to know."

Kevin was being a bitch, man—and very sarcastic with me, too. I forced a smile. "Yeah, it is good to know. You gone think what you wanna think about me, but I'm not a bad person."

"Hey, I didn't say you were." Kevin threw his hands in the air. Man, I had to defend myself, because no telling what bad shit James was out there saying about me. He had a way of spinning a situation to make himself look like the victim. "If you feeling guilty about something, that ain't for me to judge."

"Man, I gotta go," I finally said to him. This conversation was going nowhere fast. The way I saw it, I didn't owe Kevin no explanation for my actions or decisions. I was a grown-ass man. "But I appreciate your concern."

"No problem," he said to me with a smirk on his face. "And don't worry. Your lil' secret is safe with me on campus."

He left me standing there in the cold with a bundle of nerves. I couldn't believe my life, man. I had a woman accusing me of raping her. Me and James were heading in the wrong direction. And now some gay dude on campus knew of my biggest secret. I really had the loose bowels. The shit was literally knocking up against my ass.

"Hey, dude. Where you off to so fast?" Steve stopped me in the hallway outside of the bathroom.

"I gotta shit, man," I said to him with my hand on the door. "I'll catch up with you later."

"You rushed out of class earlier," he said. Steve was a nosey lil' bastard. I definitely had to watch him. Since the two of us met at the smoker, he was always up in my grille. Every step or move I made, there was that nigga up in my face. I hated the fact that I even had Mr. Poindexter's class with him. "Is everything okay, dude?"

"Man, I gotta shit," I said. "I'll holla at you."

"I'll wait for you out here," he said. I gave him a confused look. You know, like I couldn't believe this nigga was actually gone wait for me to take a shit. "We gotta meet up with the frat. Reggie just called me on my cell and told me to bring you up to the big house."

"Fuck," I kept saying over and over again to myself while on the toilet. I finally had time to release myself, but I didn't feel all that relieved. There was no telling what that nigga Reggie wanted with me. "Fuck, man."

9

James

"Ms. Greene walked off the job!" I dropped my purse on top of one of the students' desks inside of Ms. Swaign's classroom. First day back on the job and she was giving me the lowdown. Ms. Swaign was the only one up at that school who gave a damn about me besides those kids. She had my back and I had hers, too.

"Yes, she did," Ms. Swaign said with a frown. She was walking through the aisles in a pair of high-heel pumps for your mama honey, picking up paper off the floor and pushing chairs underneath the desk. You know, getting ready for her students that would be rushing through the door at eight-thirty sharp.

"She couldn't control her class, and your friend Ms. Doggett was giving the poor woman bad evaluations," she continued, pulling at her long, black hair as if it was her pride and joy. Ms. Swaign was a true diva with sexy legs and a body on her that would make Halle Berry cringe with jealousy. Ms. Girl could dress, too. Sported nothing but designer this or that. I guess that was why we were such good girlfriends. I loved myself a beautiful black woman who was confident in herself and knew how to dress, honey.

"Oh, that scandalous bitch," I said, clutching my purse and heading for the door. My class was right across the hallway from Ms. Swaign's. I was preparing myself for a long and difficult day. Although those students gave Ms. Greene a hard time, they loved her at the same time. And I could only imagine how unhappy and guilty they felt now that she was gone. "She's been hoping to get rid of Ms. Greene somehow, anyway. They knew that woman was easygoing and couldn't handle a class filled with high-risk students. They set her up for failure. But I guess Ms. Greene had the good sense to quit before she got the ax. That's a shame, but Ms. Bitch gone get what's coming to her one day."

"And she also put a couple of other teachers on probation," Ms. Swaign said, writing an assignment on the board. She was one well-prepared and organized teacher. Ms. Bitch, Sheila, couldn't touch Ms. Swaign. She was one of the best teachers at that school—next to me, of course.

Ms. Swaign was thorough, honey. Every student in her class was on the honor roll. She pushed and uplifted her students. Inspirational phrases were posted all around her classroom. There was a quote above the blackboard in large black letters from the poet Dr. Maya Angelou that said simply, "You are the hope and the dream of the slave."

"And here I thought I was the only one she hated," I said,

standing in the hallway and continuing our conversation about Ms. Greene walking out on her job. Students were quickly crowding the corridors, and there were several teachers standing around and waiting. It was part of early-morning duty. Every teacher had to stand in the hallway and greet the students upon arrival. "But I guess not."

"Enough about that," said Ms. Swaign. She lowered her voice to a whisper. "So, what's going on with you and Mr. Johnny?"

I suddenly felt nauseated at the mention of my ex's name. Johnny was not one of my favorite people these days. His bad attitude and mistreatment of me at his grandma's party had really turned me completely off. If it had not been for Mookie and his friend Kevin, I don't know what I would have done. I couldn't eat or sleep. They fed me and surrounded me with love and support.

And Kevin had been very nice and sweet to me, but it was completely on a friendship level. Although I had kissed him to make Johnny jealous, there was no chemistry between us. Kevin was a girl, honey. We both were looking for dick. Period. He was a good, caring friend though, calling and checking on me throughout the day, I guess making sure I hadn't slit my wrists or anything. Everyone close to me knew I was on the verge of a nervous breakdown, even Ms. Swaign.

At home, Mookie and Kevin looked out for me, but at school, it was Ms. Swaign who held me up with love and genuine concern. When most of them teachers tried to rally together to get me fired for wearing high-heel pumps, Ms.

Swaign stood up for me in one of our after-school meetings. She told those teachers, along with Ms. Doggett and Mr. Johnson, that it was unfair the way they were treating me, that I was a human being who deserved to be treated with respect.

"Chile, he's still tripping with me," I said to her. Ms. Swaign was the only teacher at that school who I would share my personal business with. Something about her I just always trusted. Maybe it was because she knew how to coordinate the right pumps with the perfect outfit. But for real though, Ms. Swaign was sweet and I loved her spirit. "Blaming me for everything that's gone wrong in our relationship."

"Don't let him turn things on you," Ms. Swaign warned. She had been married to a fine-ass lawyer for three years. He treated her good, too, like the special lady she was. "You know men are good for doing that."

"Don't worry," I assured her. "He's dealing with an experienced bitch, honey. I ain't gone lie down and let no man walk all over me for too long. My mama, Flo, ain't raised no doormat. But let me get in this class, honey, and get ready for these kids."

"Just watch your back," Ms. Swaign had said to me with a serious look on her face. She was so worried about me. "Because you know Sheila is on the warpath and still trying to figure out a way to get rid of you for good."

And that was all of a reminder I needed. I quickly put on my game face. There was no way I was gone let Ms. Bitch, Sheila, beat me out of a job. She may have caused problems in my personal life, but I was not going to let her take me down on all fronts. One thing I knew how to do was run a classroom. With or without Ms. Greene, I could handle those students. They loved and respected me. And, as I had predicted, they missed me the week I was gone. You should have seen how happy those students were to see me standing in that doorway, honey.

"What's up, Ms. J?" Todd asked. He had a huge smile on his face. "Glad to see you back."

"It's good to see you, too, Todd," I said to him with a tight grin. You couldn't be too friendly with those students. They would take your kindness as a sign of weakness. That was how Ms. Greene lost her job: being too nice with them. Besides, Todd was one of the school's troublemakers. He'd been suspended for fighting and cutting classes, so I had to be really tough with him, otherwise Todd would have run completely over me. "There's a journal-entry assignment on the board. Take your seat and get started."

"Darn, Ms. J," he said, shaking his head, "you putting a nigga straight to work."

"That's why you're here," I reminded him, "to do work so you can grow up and be somebody."

"Oh, you got jokes," he said, "but you still cool with me, Ms. J."

I pointed at the board. Todd took his seat and immediately started his journal entry. I stole the journal entry idea from Ms. Swaign. Her students started the morning writing about something personal going on in their lives. The journal entry was simple: Tell me what's on your mind today. Sometimes it's important to know what those kids are feeling and thinking. I feel like we don't listen to them enough, anyway.

"Hey, Ms. J." Tonya ran up and hugged me around the waist. She caught me off guard with her excitement. It wasn't like we had always gotten along. Don't get me wrong. Tonya wasn't a bad student, but she had a problem with respecting authority. She was too grown and sassy and didn't know how to stay in a child's place. But, you know, I put her ass in check from day one. And we'd had an understanding between us ever since. "Welcome back. You know things ain't been quite the same around here since you left."

One thing I didn't like about Tonya though was her name. It reminded me of this ghetto chick back in New Orleans who caused me and Johnny a lot of trouble when we first got out of jail. Tonya was the one who told Johnny's cousin Kojack he was gay and Kojack went on a shooting spree. And you know the rest of the story. As much as I tried to shake the past, there was always something small in the present taking me back. For some reason I couldn't shake Johnny out of my system although he wanted nothing to do with me. Moving on is so hard to do when you really love a man. I know somebody out there could feel me.

Once the entire class was settled in their seats, I closed the door and got straight down to business. "So what happened while I was gone?" I wanted to hear their side of the story about what happened with Ms. Greene. "And why y'all think Ms. Greene quit?"

"Because they wouldn't listen to the woman," said Tonya. The class booed her.

"Okay," I said as I quickly got things under control. "We ain't gone have none of that on my watch. We gone respect each other in here. Now go ahead, Tonya."

"Thank you, Ms. J," Tonya said, rolling her eyes. "Like I was saying though, Ms. Doggett was monitoring the class and Ms. Greene was trying to teach us a lesson, but nobody was paying attention. They were being loud and ignorant and that's what happened. She got a bad evaluation and said she was tired of this shit and walked out the door."

"So, basically, y'all responsible for that woman quitting her job?" I said, shaking my head. "And all of you should feel bad, because that woman cared about each one of you. But y'all took advantage of her kindness."

"Everyone told her we were sorry," Todd said. "And promised that we would do better if she stayed, but she just walked out on us."

"Who was teaching y'all after Ms. Greene left?"

"Some substitute, but she was all old and talked like she had a frog in her throat," Shawn said, imitating a frog's voice. The entire class laughed.

Shawn was the class clown, and I had never gotten along with him from day one. The problem with Shawn was that he thought he was so smart and funny, but he was really ignorant. And he was a bully. I really couldn't stand him, but I tried my hardest not to show it.

"And what happened to this substitute?"

"They ran her off," Tonya said. "Poor woman didn't last a day."

"And we'll get rid of you, too," Shawn said without blinking.

He was staring me directly in my face when he said it, too. Baby, that lil' boy was a trip. "So, don't get too comfortable up there."

You could suddenly hear a pen drop. No one could believe that Shawn was actually challenging me. They knew of my reputation of being a no-nonsense bitch who didn't tolerate disrespect around that school. But instead of attacking Shawn, I decided to keep my cool with him. One thing about this teaching thing, you could never get too emotional with the students or take what they said personally. Otherwise you would be a basket case. Thank God I had tough skin. Being gay and growing up in the projects most of my life prepared me for just about anything.

"So I guess I don't have to ask what's on your mind," I said, cracking a joke to soften the tension between us. The class got a real kick out of it, too. Everyone was laughing. "You plotting on how to get rid of me already and I'm just getting back?"

"Don't pay him any mind, Ms. J," said Todd. "You know we got your back."

"Thanks, Todd," I said. I'm glad that for every Shawn there was a Todd. Otherwise, I would have really hated my job. "Why don't you read from your journal?"

"All I said was that I'm sad about Ms. Greene, but I'm happy you're still here," Todd said. "And that I hope we can finish the year out on a positive note, you know, man, and show everyone that we aren't all bad or dumb."

"That was really nice and I believe with hard work y'all can do just that," I said, staring out at the students and trying to contain my emotions. Some days I could actually feel their pain and frustration. Kids go through so much these days and they bring all of that stuff with them to school. I could feel what they were going through because I had been there myself. But sometimes that shit would be overwhelming even for a strong-ass bitch like me. "Okay, everybody, take out your reading books."

"Wait," I heard a soft voice say from the back of the classroom. It was Lester–the class nerd; at least that was what the other students called him. He was a skinny lil' black kid with round frames who rarely said a word in class. "I would like to read something I wrote."

"Okay. I'm sorry," I said. "Go ahead."

"Well, it's more like a poem," Lester said. "Is that okay?"

"I love poetry," I said. "So go for it. In fact, why don't you come to the front of the class?"

At first, Lester hesitated. He was very shy and scared of too much attention on him. The kids picked on Lester for being smart.

"I don't know," Lester said, pushing his glasses up on his nose. "Can I just stand at my desk and read?"

"That's fine," I said. "Everybody give Lester a hand clap for being brave enough to read his poem out loud for us."

The entire class gave him thunderous applause. Sometimes all our kids need is a lil' encouragement, honey, 'cause baby Lester started reading that poem like he was one of those poets on Russell Simmons's poetry jam. He took us by surprise with the power of his words and the drama in his voice:

"I look all around and I see all this killing,
gang banging, drug dealing, dope pushing,
gloom and doom in the chaos of wannabe
cool fools; running and knocking down my
street like I'm the next one to groom for death
coming soon, and then I see no hope in a grieving
generation of endless dreams and possibilities
and then to see the same sad story being played
out with my family of kin, fighting in a battle
of sin, and I say, A Change Must Come."

By the time Lester was finished, the entire class was on their feet and cheering, honey. Lester showed all of them haters at that school just how talented he was, and nobody was more proud of him than me.

"Lester, can I speak with you for a minute?" I said to him when class was being dismissed for the day. The words in Lester's poem made me curious about him. You know, about what was going on in his personal life at home. In a way, I felt like Lester was crying out for attention and I wanted to help him.

"Am I in trouble?" he asked shyly.

"No, you're not in any trouble." I sat at one of the students' desks and motioned for him to sit beside me. "I just wanted to chat with you. Is that okay?"

"I guess."

"I really liked that poem," I said. "And I just wanted you to know if there's anything on your mind that you wanted to talk to me about, you can."

Lester stared at the floor. I could sense he had a lot on his mind, so I continued, "It's really okay, Lester. I've been where you are."

And before I knew what was even happening, honey, Lester was crying. He had big raindrop tears falling from his eyes. It took everything in me not to cry with him.

"Go ahead and let it out," I said, rubbing his hand. You know, trying to calm his nerves. Lester was bawling and crying so hard he had snot running from his nose. "Sometimes a good cry is all we need. Here, wipe your face."

I handed him a napkin out of my purse. After a while, he just sat there and stared out in the distance. I could tell Lester was really struggling and hurting inside, so I didn't want to push.

"I gotta go." He quickly stood up to leave. There was fear in his eyes. "My daddy is probably waiting for me downstairs."

"Okay then." I walked him to the door. "But know that I'm here anytime you would like to talk to me."

"Thanks, Ms. J," he said, wiping his face with the napkin.

"Come here and give me a hug."

Lester grabbed and hugged me like he was falling off a cliff. It was really sad. What that child was missing from his life was love. So I wrapped my arms around Lester and told him that everything was going to be okay. It was an innocent and tender moment between us. Next thing you know, I hear screaming.

"Get your hands off my son!" a man shouted from the door to the classroom. He was Mr. Toole, Lester's daddy—a big, tall, black man wearing overalls. Mr. Toole had a towering presence that even scared the hell out of me. "You faggot!"

"Dad, Ms. J was just talking to me," Lester immediately tried to explain. But I could tell by the look in Mr. Toole's eyes that he wasn't trying to hear it. I had seen that look in the eyes of many people on the street. It was hatred and disgust because of who I am or the way I choose to carry myself. "That's all. I swear."

"He's right, Mr. Toole," I quickly spoke up for myself. Mr. Toole was approaching me. Oh, my God. I couldn't believe this was happening. But life is strange in that way. One minute you can be at peace and then something can come along and throw your entire world into total chaos. "I would never do anything—"

"Don't ever put your hands on my son again." Mr. Toole punched me so hard I fell across one of the desks and landed on the floor. My jaw felt broken. I could feel a couple teeth coming loose. First Johnny's brother, now Mr. Toole—getting my ass beat down was becoming routine for me. I must have lost my touch. "Let's go, son."

Lester stood there in shock, staring at me on the floor. Mr. Toole was by the door.

"Now!" Mr. Toole shouted, and all I remember was poor Lester running out of the door like a scared and lost puppy before I blacked out into la-la land.

10

Sheila

"Accusing someone of rape is a very serious matter," Dr. Abney cautioned me. I was having a very uncomfortable afternoon therapy session. I had always thought that your therapist was supposed to be on your side, but it seemed like this woman was against me from the start. Everything was my fault. Her whole tone and demeanor was making me uneasy and defensive. Hell, I was beginning to wonder why I was even paying her in the first place. "We are talking about a man's freedom, and this is not something to take lightly."

"Are you accusing me of lying?" I asked her without remorse. "Because, Dr. Abney, I cannot tell you how it makes me feel to have you questioning my integrity."

"Of course I'm not calling you a liar." She quickly softened her tone with me, leaned forward in her chair, and stared me straight in the eyes. "I'm just trying to get to the bottom of what happened that night. You had been drinking, and sometimes alcohol can cloud our judgment and reasoning."

The last couple of days had been a nightmare. I felt like someone had taken over my body like in that movie *Body Snatchers*. Getting drunk at a fund-raiser for work was one thing, but waking up naked next to a man and having no recollection of the experience was totally outrageous and unlike me.

Of course I found Johnny attractive, but there are lots of black men who are sexy to me; that doesn't mean I would ever go to bed with some of them. Johnny was gay, and I couldn't imagine allowing myself to go there with him, especially without a condom. He said it was my idea. But the truth was: Johnny took advantage of me when I was at my most vulnerable. Hell, I was drunk and he must have known I wasn't thinking clearly. Although Johnny had called numerous times trying to defend his position, I wasn't interested in speaking with him now or anytime in the future for that matter. Johnny Lomack was a name I just wanted to erase from my memory bank.

And the only reason I hadn't gone to the police was because I had been drinking and was trying to take some responsibility for what may or may not have happened that night. But there was no mistake about it: Johnny was to blame for this ordeal, and no amount of therapy 101 was going to convince me otherwise.

"Why don't you relax and have a drink of water?" Dr. Abney said as she handed me a bottle of cold water out of a small refrigerator beside her desk. Her office came equipped with everything. There was also a lounge area with a popcorn machine and television. "I don't want you to feel overwhelmed. That isn't good for anybody."

I took a long pull from the bottle and exhaled. "Thank you. I definitely needed that."

"Why don't you tell me how you felt that night after you ran into your ex-husband?"

I sat the bottle of water on top of Dr. Abney's desk and gave her a strange look. "What does Ken have to do with any of this?"

"I don't know," she said. "That's what I'm trying to understand. Just trust me for a moment. Tell me what you were feeling after running into Ken."

I stared out the window for a brief moment. Although Dr. Abney knew all of the twisted details surrounding my split from Ken, it was still very difficult for me to even go there with her without getting emotional.

"Take your time," said Dr. Abney. She sensed my reluctance. "I have nowhere to go, but I can imagine seeing him with another woman must have felt weird."

"I was very hurt," I finally admitted. My voice began to crack. I must have had a pained expression on my face, because Dr. Abney was frowning and looking sympathetic. "How could he throw some pregnant bitch in my face? My God, all I wanted was to make that man happy. Don't you think I wanted to give him a child? Finding out that we couldn't have children was hard on me, too. But I didn't give up on us—he did!"

At this point, I had tears rolling off my cheeks. My response to Dr. Abney's question had frightened me. I had no idea there were still so many unresolved feelings inside of me regarding Ken.

Dr. Abney handed me a tissue. "Here, take this and let's take a breath."

She exhaled and I followed her lead. And it felt good to simply let go and not worry about what anyone else thought. I had spent so much time trying to pretend to have it all together and put up a strong front at work that I had forgotten to take care of Sheila. What I was learning from Dr. Abney was that it wasn't a good idea to hold on to painful experiences because what you keep in can ultimately destroy you.

"Is it safe to say that you've been disappointed by black men in your life?" Dr. Abney caught me completely off guard with her line of questioning. Being that she wasn't a sister, it just sounded weird.

I wiped the remaining tears from my eyes. "Well, you know better than anyone that I haven't had a lot of success in relationships with men."

"How did you feel when you learned that your father, who you adored, had betrayed your mother with a younger woman?"

"I was angry at him, too," I said. "I just don't understand men and why they are such dogs."

"You think that most black men disrespect and take advantage of black women?"

"Yes, I do," I said without flinching. "They take advantage of us and don't think about nobody's feelings but their own. I hate how they get away with everything, too. They move from one woman to the next and there are no consequences for their actions."

"You hate them?"

"Yes, I hate them." I started off mildly, and before long I was screaming it. "I hate them! Yes, I hate them!"

"Okay," Dr. Abney said with both her hands folded on the desk. She stared at me real hard. "I think we should stop here for now. We covered a lot of ground. However, I do have a recommendation that you might not like."

"And what's that?"

"You should talk to Johnny."

"No way," I said. "I have nothing to say to that man."

"You need to deal with this situation head-on," said Dr. Abney. "Stop repressing your feelings and confront the problem, otherwise it will eat at you."

Suddenly, there was a knock at the door. At first, I was glad for the interruption. Dr. Abney was pushing me beyond my comfort zone and I was really ready to leave her office and get back to work.

"What the hell is she doing here?" I wanted to know as soon as I saw Tiffany at the door. As usual, she was in jogging pants and tennis shoes. I figured Tiffany was probably heading to the gym as early afternoon was her workout time. "You invited her to my session? Isn't that unethical?"

Tiffany stood by the door without saying a word while Dr. Abney grabbed her purse off the desk.

"I did not and would never share our conversations with

anyone," said Dr. Abney. She took off her eyeglasses and slid them inside her jacket. "I think the two of you need to talk on a friendship level. I'm off to lunch."

"Good seeing you, Doc," Tiffany said to Dr. Abney on her way out. They went back a long ways. Tiffany had been her client for over ten years. "And thank you for calling me."

"No problem, Tiffany," said Dr. Abney. "I'm glad I was able to help. Take care."

Dr. Abney left me alone with the traitor. I clutched my purse underneath my arm and prepared to leave myself.

"It's so good to see you," said Tiffany. She sounded so sincere that it was hard being mean to her. "I've been trying to reach you since the other night."

"Sorry, I've been preoccupied," I said, fumbling in my purse and trying to avoid eye contact with her. "But it's good to see you, too."

She stood directly in front of me; touched my arm. I stared at her. "I love you and I'm so sorry for everything. You have to forgive me. I missed you, Sheila."

"I don't know what you want me to say," I said to her. "But maybe when I tell you what I had to do this week you'll understand why I'm still so angry."

"What's going on?" she asked, rubbing my arm. Tiffany knew me almost better than I knew myself. She could sense something was wrong. "Talk to me."

"I had to go and get an HIV test," I said, "because of Johnny. That man has caused me nothing but stress since he entered my life."

"What happened?" she asked.

"It's a long story, but thank God the test came back negative. I don't have time to get into the details right now." I was short and cold. "But I don't blame you. I blame myself."

"Sweetie, if you ever need to talk," she said, "I'm here for you. You know that."

I clutched my purse underneath my arm. "I have to go."

Out of the blue, Tiffany grabbed hold of me. She grabbed me and placed her arms around me. And a hug from her was exactly what I needed, although I was too stubborn to ever admit it. I realized how much I had missed my friend.

"Ms. Doggett, I'm glad you're here," Ms. Edith, my secretary, said to me as I entered the office. Sometimes she got on my last good nerve. Ms. Edith had a whining voice that lingered. It was quite annoying, but the woman was efficient and that was all that mattered in the end. I rewarded a good work ethic and professionalism. "There's someone waiting to see you."

"A parent?" I asked her, looking over the daily attendance sheets. My work began soon as I arrived at the school. There was a never a dull moment.

"I think so," she said. Ms. Edith looked quite small sitting behind her desk. She was a tiny woman who wore a curly afro wig from the seventies and thick round glasses. Looking at her always gave me the giggles. I know that must sound horrible, but it's true. "He said it was important."

"Just what I need," I said, "with the day I'm having."

"Should I hold your calls?" asked Ms. Edith.

I ignored her, not because my mom didn't raise me with good manners, but, rather, because I suddenly had a strange feeling about who the unknown visitor in my office might be and that was the only thing on my mind.

And, unfortunately, I was right.

"Johnny, what are you doing here?"

He was standing in my office, pacing the floor. He must have heard me talking with Ms. Edith in the outer office.

"I needed to talk to you," he said. Johnny's voice was hoarse and he looked tired. There were large bags underneath his eyes as if he hadn't slept in days. I recognized the signs all too well, having been initiated into a sorority myself. Johnny was in the midst of pledging, and that could be quite rigorous on any soul. "You weren't returning my calls. Man, I been worried out of my mind."

I plopped down behind my desk and sat my purse on the table behind me. Since Johnny was up in my face—in my office—I could no longer run from the issues between us. So I decided to take Dr. Abney's advice and confront him head-on. "Why don't you have a seat?"

He sat down in the chair with a nervous grin on his face. "You look good," he said.

"Thank you." I was cold. You know, I didn't want him to get the wrong idea. This was not a social call. I meant business. "I've been thinking about what happened—"

He cut me off. "So have I." Johnny had to strain his voice just to talk. "I can't sleep. Man, what you accused me of the other night has been eating me up inside."

"Well, I'm sorry if I caused you to miss any sleep," I said very sarcastically. Johnny was the typical man, selfishly thinking about his own feelings. "But this hasn't been easy for me either. I have been trying to deal with this situation as best I can. Whether you believe me or not, I honestly can't remember what happened that night."

"So, what you saying?" asked Johnny. He had a perplexed, worried expression on his face. "You still think I raped you?"

"I shouldn't have accused you of that," I said to put his mind at ease. "I know I had been drinking and several people told me I was drunk. So let's just put this awful experience behind us and move on with our lives."

Johnny stared at me real hard with tears in his eyes. "I would never hurt you, or any woman, intentionally. Man, you gotta believe me on that."

"Look, Johnny, you're obviously a nice guy." I tried to keep my composure and not give in to my emotions. The truth was I had some feelings for Johnny. He got under my skin more than I cared to admit. "But I think in light of everything that has happened, we should keep our distance."

"So, basically, you don't wanna have anything else to do with a nigga?" asked Johnny. He actually sounded hurt.

I stood up from behind my desk, being very professional but signaling for him to leave. "I don't mean to be rude, but I do have a lot of work to do."

Johnny made his way to the door without putting up much resistance. "No problem. I understand. Thanks for hearing me out though."

"Sorry to interrupt, Ms. Doggett." Ms. Edith swung the door open on us. Although she was a sweet woman, this was one quality I hated about her—how she would enter my office without knocking.

"Ms. Edith, I'm still in a conference," I said to her. "What did I tell you about knocking first?"

"I'm so sorry, ma'am," she said, "but Mr. Toole is here with his son, Lester, claiming that the boy was sexually molested by Mr. Santiago."

"What?" I heard the words come out of Ms. Edith's mouth, but I still couldn't believe it. Johnny stared at me in disbelief. I regained my composure. "Ms. Edith, I'm still in a meeting and this is a matter we should discuss in private."

"Well, he must have made some mistake," said Johnny. He went into defense mode. And if I had any doubts up until that moment that Johnny really cared about James, his true feelings surfaced at the sign of someone he loved being threatened. "James would never hurt anybody, especially a kid."

"I'm going to have to ask you to leave," I immediately said to Johnny. There was suddenly so much tension in the room that it was giving me a headache. "This is a school matter."

Ms. Edith, Johnny, and I walked out into the front office where Mr. Toole and Lester were sitting and waiting for me. When Johnny saw Mr. Toole, he couldn't contain himself. He went at the man.

"I don't know what kind of game you're playing, homey," he said to Mr. Toole. Poor Lester looked scared behind his round frames. Ms. Edith and I were taken by surprise as well. "But James ain't do nothin' to your son."

"What the fuck you gotta do with this?" Mr. Toole stood up to confront Johnny. Both of them sent my pressure through the roof.

"Absolutely nothing," I said. I stood between the two of them before the situation could get any uglier–if that was even possible. "Johnny was just leaving."

Johnny shook his head as if he was in shock and then glanced around the room at me, Ms. Edith, Mr. Toole, and Lester. I don't know what was going through his mind, but he had me worried big-time.

"Please don't make me call security," I warned.

"All right, man." Johnny threw both of his arms into the air and made a quick exit. "I'm outta here."

"Mr. Toole, please come into my office," I quickly said. He and Lester followed close behind me. Before entering my office, I had one final set of instructions for Ms. Edith. This was a highly sensitive matter that would deserve my full attention. Although I had wanted to get rid of James, there was nothing gratifying about this situation. We were talking about an innocent child, and I couldn't find any satisfaction at Lester's expense. However, this was what I had been afraid of all along, having someone like James dealing with the student population, particularly our young boys. "Don't let anyone interrupt us and hold all my calls."

"Yes, Ms. Doggett." Ms. Edith sounded nervous. She must have weighed the enormity of the situation for herself. "Should I try to locate Mr. Johnson at home? He's out on personal leave."

"Yes, please do," I said, "and tell him to drop whatever he's doing and get to my office immediately."

11

Johnny

"Johnny, what are you doing?" James wanted to know as soon as he saw me walking through the door of his classroom. "And why are you even here?"

Man, when I found James it was a sad sight to see. His face was completely bruised and he had a black eye. Some woman was hugging and trying to comfort him. Some woman who was so beautiful she looked like she should have been on the cover of *Essence* magazine or something. And by the look on James's face, I knew he was shocked to see me. Both of them were.

"What happened to your face?" I asked him. Seeing him all beat up like that was tearing me up inside. Man, of course I still loved James. No matter what happened between us I couldn't stand the idea of someone hurting him. I was ready to kick somebody's ass up in that school for real. "Who did this to you?"

"I can't deal with you right now." James left me standing

there with that woman. He just walked away and started staring out the window. James was giving me the silent treatment.

"Hi, I'm Ms. Swaign," the mysterious woman finally extended her hand and said. The bracelets around her arms jingled as we shook hands over a friendly smile. "I'm one of the teachers at the school and a good friend of James. It's so nice to finally meet you. Maybe we should step out in the hall and talk. Give him some time alone."

Me and Ms. Swaign stepped away for a moment, leaving James standing by the window. Although he was acting shitty with me, I was trying not to let it get to me. At that moment, I knew his ass needed me even if his stubbornness wouldn't allow him to admit it.

"What happened?" I asked. It was after school hours and most of the students and faculty had already left for the day, but there were still a few teachers in the building, walking through the halls.

"Apparently, one of his students' parents assaulted him," Ms. Swaign explained.

"That son of a bitch." I cut her off. "He put his hand on James?"

"You're already aware of the situation?" asked Ms. Swaign in a very low whisper. I guess she didn't want anyone to know what was going on. From what James had told me, most of the teachers up at that school didn't like him, and we weren't trying to give them any ammunition to use against James either.

"I met that fool in the office a few minutes ago," I explained to her. "This is not good. This is not good at all. But there's no way James touched that lil' boy."

"Look, they have been trying to get rid of him for a long time," Ms. Swaign said, giving it to me straight. I could tell she really cared about James, too. "And I would not be surprised if this is some kind of setup."

"Well, believe me, they ain't gone get away with it," I assured her. "Not by a long shot."

Ms. Swaign stared at her watch. "Damn it, I have to pick my daughter up from day care. But I hate to leave him like this."

"You go ahead," I said. "I'll look out for him."

"I'm glad you're here," she said, rubbing my arm. "He really misses you. Let him know I'll call later."

I waited until Ms. Swaign disappeared down the hallway before reentering the classroom. Man, it was just my way of buying time. I knew this was not going to be an easy conversation. Beside the horrible issue at hand, me and James had some deep personal shit going on between us.

"Your friend had to leave," I said to him. James was still standing by the window with his arms folded across his chest. "She said she'll call you later. You know she's really worried about you. And so am I."

James turned to face me with a bitter look. "You never answered me earlier. Why are you here? Or do I even have to ask. You were here to see your new best friend, Sheila."

"I'm worried about you right now," I said. "I ran into that

man downstairs and he's accusing you of some real serious shit. What happened?"

"Why are you avoiding the question?" James pushed. "Were you here to see Sheila?"

"Yeah, I was here to see her," I said with a straight face, but the truth was: I felt guilty as hell. This was the first time I had seen James since me and Sheila had fucked around. And I felt bad, man. Real bad. You know, having cheated on James with someone else. I know we weren't "officially" together at the time, but it still bothered the hell out of me. "I had to talk to her about something, but it's no big deal."

"No big deal." James got an immediate attitude. Although he was tearing into my ass like a bolt of electricity, all I wanted to do was put my arms around him. Maybe it was the black eye that was getting to a nigga. But I felt sorry for James. And he needed me to take care of him, and I wanted to for the first time in a long while. "You have been treating me like shit for weeks and I'm supposed to just brush it off. You better get the fuck out of my face for real. And I ain't playing with you either."

"So, you gone be like that," I said, trying to flip the switch on him. Make him feel guilty for the way he was now treating me. Some of this shit was a game, man, and I was always ready and willing to play it. But my feelings for James—now that was real. "Just close the door in my face."

"Isn't that what you did to me the other night at your grandma's birthday party?" James walked over to his desk and started looking through a bunch of papers. You know, trying to appear like he was suddenly so busy. "Just let yourself out before we both say something we regret."

I walked over and stood in front of the desk. "I ain't going no-fucking-where. We gone talk about this whether you want to or not."

"No we're not either!" he shouted in my face. The anger in his voice hit me in the chest like a bow and arrow. Man, I had really hurt James, and at that moment I was just beginning to realize how much. "Just get the hell out of my face and go back to your lil' fraternity. That's all that matters to you anyway."

"See, that's the problem." I pointed at him. "You never understood what was important to me!"

"Whatever." He waved his hand in the air and continued looking at the papers on the desk. Man, I don't know what suddenly got into me, but I knocked all of that shit off his desk. I swept those papers and books off James's desk like I was dusting furniture.

"Are you insane or something?" James stared at me in shock. He hadn't seen that side of me in a long time. Last time I had gotten that angry, we were inside the pen and some nigga tried to test my manhood. I beat the dude's ass to a pulp and ended up in the hole for weeks. "Knocking shit off my desk."

"Do you think our relationship has been easy on me?" I finally went there with James, expressing to him stuff that had been on my mind for months.

He stared at me, rolling his eyes. But I continued anyway. "Having my brothers and everybody looking at me like I'm some freak. This shit ain't easy, man! I'm trying to be with you and still be a man. So for once stop thinking about yourself and think about me."

"Are you finished?" he asked without blinking an eye. James was being so cold and bitter with me that it was catching a nigga completely off guard. It sounded like he didn't have love for me anymore, and that scared me more than anything. "Because I have work to do."

"Man, I'm outta here." I threw both my arms in the air and opened the door, but Sheila and two school security guards pumped my brakes. They pumped my brakes and backed my ass up inside the classroom. They were coming to get James: a white and a black security guard. Man, I couldn't believe this shit.

"James, I'm sorry to have to do this to you, especially here," Sheila said with regret. Although she didn't like James, I could sense this was not easy for her. She was not getting any pleasure from this ordeal. "But Mr. Toole is accusing you of molesting his son and you're going to have to come down to my office."

"Am I under arrest?" asked James.

"No, you're not," Sheila said with the two officers posted beside her. If they weren't planning an arrest, they for damn sure looked like they wanted to. "We just simply need for you to come down to the office so we can talk."

"This is a mistake," James said as he gathered some items from his desk. "I ain't even do nothing."

Man, things were going down so fast, I could hardly keep up. One minute me and my nigga were fighting and the next thing he was being hauled off to the main office for molestation charges.

"I'm innocent," said James as they walked him out the door. He looked scared, man, but tried to remain cool. James seemed more worried about me than anything else. "This is all one big mistake, so don't even worry about me."

And they suddenly disappeared into thin air so that the incident felt surreal and unbelievable. After they left, all I could do was stand there in shock and amazement like a block of ice froze my ass in time.

"They're accusing my boy of molesting someone!" Ms. Flo, James's mama, shouted over the phone in my ear. I knew telling her the news wasn't gone be easy. One thing about Ms. Flo—she loved her son to death. This woman didn't play when it came to somebody messing with her children. "What the hell for?"

I was standing on the yard with the phone up to my ear and looking around for Kevin. I was looking for Kevin so he could put me in touch with James's friend Mookie. "They trying to say he molested some lil' boy in his class."

"Oh, they're motherfucking lying." Ms. Flo said. I forgot to mention she was ghetto, too. I mean straight-up hood. "If they think they gone pin some shit like this on my boy, they got another thing coming. I'm on my way up there on the first thing smoking out of Nawlins."

And that was the last thing I remembered hearing from

Ms. Flo before she hung up on me. But I couldn't blame the woman. This whole situation had me upset, too. All James tried to do was look out for them children up at that school and now they wanted to hang him from the ceiling like a Negro in the Jim Crow South.

"Excuse me," I said, stopping a short, stout girl in the yard. She and Kevin had worked together on the Homecoming Fashion Show. "Have you seen Kevin?"

"Not since earlier today," she said, juggling several books in her arm. "But I think he already gone home."

"Do you have his number?" I asked. At this point, I wasn't thinking about how it might have looked for me to be asking for Kevin's number. In fact, I wasn't thinking about the frat finding out about our connection. All I could think about was my nigga sitting up in that jail and wondering how he was gone get out. They set his bail at five thousand dollars. Kevin was the only person I knew who had that kind of money on hand besides my peeps. And you know I wasn't trying to get them involved in this business.

"I sure don't," she said. "I'm sorry."

"Thanks anyway, baby," I said. I walked around the campus, going from one building to the next one. My heart was racing and I was so damn frantic, man, that it didn't make any sense.

"Johnny, wait up!" Steve shouted after me. I had seen him coming my way, so I tried to duck off behind a tree. The last thing I needed was his nosey ass up in my face. But somehow he spotted me anyway.

"Man, I don't have time to talk right now," I said, pushing

my way across campus. Steve walked and talked with me at the same time. I was walking so fast, he actually had to run to keep up with me.

"Slow down, dude," he said. "What's going on? Talk to me. I can tell something is wrong. Does it have something to do with the frat?"

"You wouldn't understand," I said. "Believe me. You wouldn't understand."

"That's cold, dude," he said. "I'm about to be your frat brother and you can't trust me?"

I stopped and stared at him. Part of me wanted to open up to Steve, because I needed someone to talk to big-time. It felt like my entire world was falling apart and I had so many thoughts running through my head.

"Talk to me, dude," he pushed.

I looked around to see who was nearby. Since the smoker, Steve and I had gotten closer. The pledging process was hard, and you needed someone to depend on for information and moral support. There was so much fraternity history to learn. Steve and I would meet up at the library and study. Whatever I didn't know, he knew, and vice versa. But still, I wasn't sure I could trust his ass with my personal business.

"Okay, let's talk," I finally said to him. "But not right here."

"Well, let's go to my dorm room," he said. "We can talk in private over there."

I followed Steve to his room and wondered what I was going to actually say to him once we arrived. This was not how I imagined coming out to him, or to anyone on campus for that matter. There was simply no way of telling Steve the truth without revealing my status to him.

"Okay. Now talk," Steve immediately said once we were inside his dorm room. He sat on top of his desk and grabbed a basketball. I noticed pictures of Michael Jordan and Kobe Bryant posted on the walls. Steve had game, but he was nowhere near the talent of his idols. "You can trust me, dude."

I sat on the bed and wondered. The cat suddenly had my damn tongue.

"Look, dude," Steve said, squeezing the basketball. He seemed nervous, too. "I kinda have a feeling what this is about. What you're trying to tell me, but scared to."

I stared at him real hard. "You do?"

"Yeah, dude." Steve stood up and looked out of his door. He wanted to make sure no one was around in the hallway. He still had the basketball in his hand. Steve was acting really strange. He closed the door and finished his thought. "I know what this is about. I had a feeling about it for a long time."

"I don't think we're on the same page," I said to him. "You have no idea what I'm talking about. Believe me."

Steve grabbed at his dick and sat on the dresser. If I didn't know any better, he was coming on to me. Man, I couldn't believe this was happening. Our school's star basketball player might be in the closet. On any other occasion this would have been a fantasy come true. You know, having a fine-ass basketball player coming out to me in his dorm room and then having hot, passionate sex with him. But, man, my mind was on a whole other level.

"I had been wanting to tell you something for a long time," he continued, "but I was afraid, too. I saw you talking to that dude Kevin the other day on campus and y'all looked kind of intense."

"Okay," I said. "And what does that have to do with you?"

Steve fumbled with the basketball, choking over his words. "I'm trying to tell you what's up with me."

"What you mean, what's up with you?" I played stupid, though the handwriting was on the wall. Opening up to Steve was going to be easier than I had thought. He was making a way for me to feel totally comfortable with him.

"Come on, dude," he said. "Do I have to spell it out?"

"Basically," I said.

"I like to fool around," he said, "and I'm not talking about with just bitches."

I nodded my head, staring at him. It was almost too good to be true. Steve was actually coming out to me in his dorm room.

"Wow, that's some revelation," I said. "But why did you choose to tell me of all people?"

Steve suddenly had a nervous grin on his face. "Like I said, I saw you talking to Kevin and figured you were down. Am I right? Are you gay, dude?"

"I don't like labels," I said, "but you're on the right track. I'm down, too."

"Word." Steve suddenly fell silent, squeezing the basketball. He wasn't giving me the reaction I had expected. Steve seemed like he was upset more than relieved.

"You don't know how good it feels to get that shit off my

chest," I said. "Felt like I was alone. It definitely helps to know someone who's going through what I'm going through."

"Look, dude." Steve tossed the basketball on the bed and grabbed one of his textbooks. He grabbed his book and opened his door. Man, this nigga was acting weird and tripping big time. "I forgot I had a lot of work to do. Why don't I catch up with you later."

I stood up to leave, looking at him in disbelief. He had my head spinning. I was confused by his reaction. Why this nigga opened up to me in the first place and was now basically throwing me out of his room? It didn't make any sense.

"You all right, man?" I asked him.

"I'm good." He cleared his throat. His body language told me otherwise. Steve was suddenly uncomfortable around me. For someone who was down with messing with dudes, he sure wasn't acting like it. "Like I said, I just have a lot of work to do."

"Shit, I didn't even get a chance to tell you what was going on with me," I said. Steve still held the door for me to leave. He wasn't even trying to hear me out. "I was trying to find Kevin because one of my friends got arrested."

"Good luck," Steve said in a dry-ass tone. This nigga didn't care one way or the other.

"I know you gotta study," I said, "so I'll holla at you later. Thanks for the talk."

"Yeah, just holla at me," he said, avoiding eye contact. Steve didn't even want to look in my direction, as if he couldn't stand the sight of me. "Peace out."

"Call me later." I was now talking to the door. Steve slammed the door in my face and left me in the hallway with a bundle of nerves. I had a lot of nervous energy and I didn't know what to do next. You know, I didn't know if I could really trust this dude. Of course, I wondered if I had just made the biggest mistake of my life, confiding in him. Man, it felt like I was losing it, but I had to stay focused on James.

With that in my mind, I took to the stairs like my life depended on it.

12

James

"Here's to getting out of jail," Mookie said with a glass raised in the air. We were upstairs at the Bachelor's Mill nightclub having cocktails and trying to forget about my problems, which were hanging over us in the smoke-filled room like a dark cloud.

The Mill was a weekend and Thursday-night spot, so on other nights you just had a few people playing pool, having drinks, and listening to the jukebox. Anita Baker was on the track telling us how sweet love is. On any other night, I probably would have agreed with Ms. Girl. But Anita caught me in a weird place and at a strange time in my life when I wasn't feeling all that loving and lovable.

"And here's to also beating those charges, too," Mookie continued, shouting over Anita Baker, "and showing them motherfuckers at that school what a bad broad you are!"

"I can drink to that," I said with a half-ass grin on my face, taking a sip from the glass and trying to get in the mood. The truth was I didn't feel much like celebrating after what I had gone through recently, honey. They're threatening to send a bitch to jail, y'all.

You heard me right, honey. Mr. Toole told Mr. Johnson and Ms. Doggett that I molested his son and he was planning on taking the matter to the police. When Toole punched me in my face, I thought that would be the end of his tirade. He gave me a black eye. If I knew his ass was gone take things further, I would have gotten up off that floor and given him a reason to put me in jail.

Mr. Toole went to my job on me, honey, telling those people I molested his son. What I look like, trying to mess with some damn lil' boy? I don't want no damn child. I'm a grown-ass man—woman, whatever you wanna call me—who fucks around with grown-ass men. I don't get down with any children. You damn right. I was angry.

Wouldn't you be if someone was accusing you of something you know you didn't do?

I couldn't and would never hurt an innocent child, let alone take advantage of one sexually. I think that's some sick shit, anyone who messes around with little children. Honey, that ain't even in my character or my spirit. I love helping children and looking out for people. That's why I got into teaching in the first place. If you couldn't tell, this situation was hurting me, y'all, like nothing else before in my life.

Ms. Doggett came to my classroom with two security guards who work up at the school, honey. And the worst part about it was that Johnny heard and saw everything. Johnny had come up to the school unexpectedly and was there when everything was going down. We were inside my classroom arguing about our relationship when those two security guards showed up with Sheila.

Of course, I didn't want Johnny to know my personal or professional business. In fact, I didn't want to see him, period. After the way he had been treating me, there was nothing for us to say to each other. And coming on my job and trying to make his case was not cool either. The truth was, Johnny didn't come up to the school to see me, anyway. He came to see, Ms. Bitch, Sheila, who was acting like she wasn't happy that I was being accused of molestation. Chile, please. That bitch had to be celebrating and jumping up and down inside. Sheila had been against me from the beginning, and this was what she always wanted: for me to be fired from the school and away from those kids.

When the security guards were escorting me to the office, I was embarrassed. And if that wasn't bad enough, y'all, Johnny looked like he pitied me. And I hate for anyone to feel sorry for me. And I felt like Sheila was winning. She already had my man, but was about to take my job away from me, too. It was a bad time for me. They took me to the office and grilled me. They asked me a thousand and one questions as if I was some damn criminal. They went all into my past. You know, having gone to prison for stealing.

"I told you Johnny still cared about you," Mookie said, looking at himself in a small compact mirror. He was such a vain girl, honey. Mookie was the type of person who couldn't pass a mirror without looking at himself in it. And you know he was smoking a joint, as usual. And I was still worried about his health. How skinny he was. You could see the bones in his body he was so little. "That boy tracked me down and I could tell he was really worried about you."

"That was guilt," I said, "not love. And he had no business calling my mama into this either. Now I gotta deal with Flo tomorrow while I'm trying to fight for my job and my good name at the same time."

Don't get me wrong. I appreciated the fact that Flo wanted to come all the way from New Orleans to be by my side. But I didn't see what she could do to help the situation. Besides, Flo had a hot temper and had a way of sometimes making a bad situation even worse.

I remember being in the tenth grade and getting into a fight with Wallace Harris. Wallace was a bully and couldn't stand my guts. He called me a punk in front of everybody in the cafeteria. Baby, I took my school plate and slammed him in the face with it. He had chicken and mashed potatoes all over his face and clothes. And we got to fighting and both our asses ended up in the office. We had a woman principal, Ms. Spears, who was really nice. She had only planned to suspend me for a few days until Flo showed up. She showed up in the woman's office, flying off at the mouth and using profanity. When Ms. Spears asked her to leave the building, Flo jumped across the desk on the woman. I ain't lying, y'all. Flo jumped on the principal and beat that woman without mercy. And you know I could never go back to that school again. They put my ass out for good. I had to bus it to another school way across town.

"Girl, you should be glad your mama coming," Mookie said, taking a puff off the joint and then a sip from his glass. He was really getting messed up that night. Mookie's eyes were already red. And by the sound of his voice, I could tell he had had too much drink. "I wish my mama was still alive. It's a blessing to have your mama's love."

Both Mookie's parents were dead. I don't know how they died, because he never would share too much about his personal life. All I knew was that his parents were dead and he didn't have much family. And the family he did have didn't want anything to do with him. Mookie said it was because he was a flaming queen. He often joked about not having family in his life, but I could tell it was hurting him. When he talked about Flo, there was a longing in his voice to be loved by family.

"Cherish the time with your mama," continued Mookie. "I think it's so cute that she accepts you for who you are. You know a lot of people don't have that with their parents."

"I agree," I finally said, warming up to the idea of Flo coming to town. "And I know it might not sound like it, but I do love my mama. I just don't want that girl doing anything crazy at that meeting tomorrow. Sometime Flo gets too emotional for me."

The school's charter board had called a private meeting with me and Mr. Toole to discuss the matter at hand. The charter board didn't want anything to get out to the public about what had supposedly happened and was hoping we could solve the matter in private. What I needed was a lawyer at that meeting, honey. Not my mama. But, nevertheless, Flo was coming to town by way of Amtrak. That girl was due to arrive early in the afternoon, only hours before my big meeting with the charter board.

"Is this just a party for two?" Kevin snuck up behind me and Mookie with a huge smile on his face. Having his support and friendship was the one bright spot in this awful situation. Kevin was a godsend.

"Hey there," I greeted him with a hug. "I'm glad you made it out tonight so I could thank you in person for posting my bail."

You heard me right, honey. Kevin paid five thousand dollars to get me out of jail, so you know I was grateful to him. That man barely knew me, but he put his money on the line for my ass. With the world the way it is these days—everybody trying to use you for something—Kevin was one of those rare people, just genuine and kind.

"No problem," he said, kissing Mookie on both cheeks. "What's up, Ms. Mookie?"

"Not much, darling," said Mookie with a cocktail in his hand. "Why don't you sit and have a drink with us?"

Kevin sat between us and we talked for hours, listening to the jukebox and getting wasted. They were doing everything in their power to try to cheer me up. But it wasn't working. For one, I couldn't get Johnny off my mind and they wouldn't let me.

"You should give that man another chance," Kevin said. We

had discussed everything from politics to fashion, but now we were back on Johnny. "When he tracked me down, I could tell he was really worried about you."

"I tried to tell her," said Mookie, "but this is a stubborn lil' bitch. She gone lose her man trying to be too prideful."

"I appreciate what y'all trying to do," I said, "but me and Johnny got a lot to work out. He hurt me real badly, and I don't know if I'm ready to open my heart up to him again."

"Well, whatever you do"–Mookie hugged me–"you know I got your back, girl."

"Tonight Gamma Phi picking their spring line," Kevin said. He had mixed feelings about the whole pledging thing. "I'm happy for him, although I won't be on that line this year."

Kevin had wanted to pledge, too, but they wouldn't accept him because he was gay. And you wonder why I'm against fraternities. Here Kevin was a good man and successful, too, and they still didn't want him. In my opinion, he was better off without them. Kevin was a respected fashion designer and had mad paper, honey. Why would he want to join an organization that would simply beat on him in the spirit of brotherhood? If he wanted an ass whipping, I could have taken him out on the street corner of any hood in America. Believe me, they would surely get the job done right.

The fact that Johnny wants to pledge a fraternity full of homophobes is beyond me, too. Most of them dudes in those frats don't like gays, and I know it for a fact. One of my good friends from New Orleans, Marvin, tried to pledge when he attended college. The brothers of this particular frat loved Marvin until they discovered he was gay. After which, they cut him off completely. I've told Johnny this story about Marvin, but he didn't wanna hear of it. It was like pledging was more important to him than anything on earth, including me. It makes me sick just thinking back to that time.

Shit, I tried to be supportive of Johnny, but I guess it wasn't enough support. You know how much he wanted to pledge that stupid fraternity. Maybe that was why Johnny left me in the first place. At least that was the impression he gave me when we were arguing inside my classroom before Ms. Bitch and the security guards showed up.

"You think Johnny gone make the line?" I asked Kevin, coughing and suddenly feeling dizzy. The liquor was getting to my head and the smoke inside the Mill was suffocating me. And the smell of smoke was all in my hair and clothes so that it was beginning to make me sick. I hated that smoky smell, but I loved coming to the Mill for their drinks. They made the strongest drinks for your mama, honey. Shit, that was why everybody came to the Mill—for the drinks and the music. It wasn't like the Mill was a first-rate, classy joint, but it had good music. And I suddenly felt like dancing. I had already had two cocktails and was feeling very lovely.

"Those frat boys love Johnny on campus," said Kevin. "I'm sure he's going to get in before anyone else."

"I'm glad to hear that." I quickly changed the topic though, bopping my head to music and snapping my fingers. The last thing I wanted to do was spend the rest of the night talking about Johnny and his frat boys. Like I said, I was feeling the music in my soul, way down in my feet. "Let's go downstairs and dance, honey."

And we did. Me, Kevin, and Mookie got on that dance floor, twirling and spinning around like three schoolgirls on a weekend getaway. The DJ mixed house music with hip hop. Although I loved hip hop, there was nothing like that old-school shit. House music, like Phyllis Hyman's, lifted me off my feet and took me to the moon.

"Feel the music, baby!" Mookie shouted at me as I kicked and twirled on the dance floor. You see, for some of us, house music was all we had to hold on to when things really got bad in our lives. I was facing molestation charges but was out dancing like I had not a care in the world. "Don't let nobody stop you from getting your life, girl!"

And I didn't let anyone stop me. I closed my eyes like Dorothy in *The Wizard of Oz* and allowed that music to sweep me away in a funnel cloud. Although I didn't know his name, the DJ saved my life that night.

"Who punched you in your face?" Flo asked as soon as she stepped off the train and saw me standing there in Union Station next to Mookie. "That's all I wanna know."

"Hey, Flo, girl." I wrapped my arms around her and held on tightly. I ain't gone even lie. I know I talked a lot of shit about my mama coming to town, but it felt so good to be in her arms again. The last time I had seen Flo was during the whole Hurricane Katrina drama. We were standing outside the Superdome with thousands of other people waiting to get bused or airlifted to another state. Both me and Flo were broke and tore down from the floor up, honey. Flo ended up in Texas, and you already know I came to DC to meet up with Johnny. "It's so good to see you. I can't believe you're really here. This my friend Mookie I was telling you about."

"Nice to meet you, Mookie, baby," Flo said, shaking hands with him and smiling, flashing two gold teeth. My mama looked good though. She came to DC in style, honey. Flo was wearing some cute jeans and sporting a fierce lil' short hairstyle. I had never seen my mama with short hair. For as long as I could remember, that girl loved long weaves hanging down her back. I use to call Flo a weave queen.

"Nice to meet you too, darling." Mookie kissed Flo on the cheek. "I heard so much about you."

"I hope all good?" Flo said, cutting her eyes at me. That girl couldn't stop staring in my direction for nothing in the world.

"Of course, that's all he talks about is his mama, Flo," said Mookie. He picked up one of Flo's bags. That girl came to town with way too much luggage. Flo had three big suitcases like she was moving to DC for good. "And how you don't take no shit off nobody."

"Don't believe him, Mookie." Flo stared at me with that worried-mother look in her eyes. I avoided eye contact with her. You know, afraid she was going to figure me out. That I was in a lot of pain over not just the molestation charges, but me and Johnny breaking up, too. I didn't want Flo all in my business right away.

"I'm sweet as pudding," she continued. "Just as long as nobody don't fuck with me or my children. Then I might have to kick somebody's ass."

"I know that's right, girl," said Mookie. "I ain't even mad at you."

"And you never answered me, mister," Flo said as she turned her attention back on me. "Who hit you in your face and gave you that black eye? I know Johnny ain't putting his hands on you up here."

"Now you're talking crazy. You know Johnny would never hit me." I picked up one of Flo's other suitcases off the ground. "But I'll explain everything in the car, girl."

"You know Johnny called me," Flo said. "He sounded really worried about you up here. I could tell how much he loves you. How y'all making out, anyway? He was all tight-lipped when I asked him."

"Maybe you should take a hint then," I said, "and stay out of grown folks' business."

"Well, excuse me, chile," said Flo. "I was just asking."

"Are you hungry?" I quickly changed the subject.

Flo rubbed her big stomach. That girl looked like she was nine months pregnant with that gut the size of the Mississippi. One thing about Flo was that she loved to get her eat on, honey.

"You know your mama a big girl, so you don't even have to ask me that. They ain't have no good food on that train."

"Well, there are a lot of places to eat inside of Union Station," I said, showing her around.

Union Station was like a minimall, with eateries, a movie theater, and a bookstore. It had a couple of cute shops, too, but those girls were too expensive for me. Most people came through Union Station if they were traveling by train, not for shopping. If someone wanted to do some serious shopping, they would head to the Pentagon City mall. Me and Mookie lived for Uno's pizza in Union Station though. Friday nights was our pizza-and-movie night.

"I want some Popeye's chicken," Flo said, turning her nose up at the eateries inside Union Station. You know you can take some people out of the hood, but you can't take the hood out of them, honey. Flo was a New Orleans girl and there was no changing her. "'Cause this lil' shit they got in here ain't gone cut it. I need some red beans and fried chicken."

I glanced at Mookie. He was now getting a glimpse of what I was talking about when it came to Flo. How that girl could be a handful, honey. But that was still my mama and I loved her to death. Make no mistake about it.

"There's a Popeye's near Mookie's apartment." We walked out of the station and headed to the car. It was early in the day, so there weren't that many people out and about, like during rush hour. Mostly working people took the train from Baltimore into DC. Let's just say you wouldn't want to be in Union

Station during that time of the day. Baby, those crowds of people were nothing nice. "We can get something to eat before heading to the meeting at the school."

"Is Johnny gone meet us later?" asked Flo.

"I don't think so," Mookie said, but I immediately cut him off. Like I said earlier, the last thing I wanted was Flo in my personal business. If she knew what was going on between me and Johnny, that would be the whole conversation while she was in town.

"Johnny has classes and finals this week," I said. "So if I was you, I wouldn't expect to see him on this trip."

As we pulled out of the Union Station parking lot, I could feel Flo staring at me from the backseat.

"I could tell something's going on with you," Flo said, lighting a cigarette. She took a puff and exhaled. Little circles of smoke floated around in the car like they were on invisible strings. "And you better believe Flo gone find out what it is before I leave this town. And I also bought my knife just in case any shit goes down at that school."

13

Sheila

"Please take a seat, Mr. Toole," Mr. Johnson said, plopping down in a chair himself. We were inside my office having a private meeting. Mr. Johnson was not happy about this situation; he had a very serious expression on his face. "Ms. Doggett and I wanted to speak with you before the meeting with the charter board members."

Mr. Toole loosened his tie. He was dressed very professional, like a man who realized the seriousness of what was at stake and the power he possessed. Our school was facing a major PR crisis if Mr. Toole went through with his allegations against James. Therefore, Mr. Johnson had come up with a plan that I wasn't completely behind. However, I loved this school and was willing to do just about anything to protect its reputation and interests.

"How are you feeling today?" I stared at Mr. Toole with an intimidating look. Although I may have had my share of problems with James, my sole purpose was getting to the truth. This was not a lynch mob, and I had no intention of pushing my agenda. If a child's rights had been violated, however, then justice should be served. But if Mr. Toole was lying out of anger and homophobia, that was unacceptable. My allegiance was to Lester—and Lester only—because he was the real victim in this situation.

Mr. Toole cleared his throat. Maybe I was staring at him too hard, because he was quite nervous. But my intention was to rattle him. "I'm good as could be expected, you know," he replied.

"Would you like a drink of water?" I asked him.

"No, thanks. I just would like to know why y'all wanted to meet with me in private."

Mr. Johnson chimed in before I could say a word. "Well, we wanted to see if there was a way we could all come to some type of resolution."

Mr. Toole frowned. "I don't understand."

"We're all thinking about the best interests of the boy," Mr. Johnson explained. He removed his eyeglasses and placed them inside his suit jacket. "This situation must be very hard on the both of you and we would like to make it as easy as possible."

"What do you have in mind?" Mr. Toole asked with a sudden glow in his eyes. He understood exactly where Mr. Johnson was heading and was simply waiting for him to get there. Word had gotten back to us from several parents in the neighborhood that Mr. Toole was thinking about suing the school. We wanted to get ahead of his lawsuit.

"We would like to settle this thing out of court," Mr. Johnson said, wiping sweat from his forehead. "So the boy won't have to endure a long and embarrassing trial. And everyone can get on with their lives."

Mr. Toole touched his chin. "How much of a settlement are you talking?"

I leaned across the desk and handed Mr. Toole a small piece of paper. He opened the paper and nodded his head in agreement.

"Just a little something to help you get through this stressful time," I said.

"I can see y'all thought a lot about my stress," Mr. Toole said as he stared at the piece of paper long and hard.

Diane Richardson had gone to our management firm and convinced them to settle with Mr. Toole for the sum of fifty thousand dollars. Advantage Principles wanted to protect their contract with the government; any negative publicity threatened their interests as well.

"So, basically, y'all trying to buy me off so I don't go to police?" asked Mr. Toole as if he was suddenly offended by our forwardness. "Forget what happened to my son."

What a crock of shit. He knew exactly what this meeting was about and he expected an offer. I could see straight through his cheesy smile and cheap cologne, which was giving me the worse damn headache in the world. Mr. Toole must have sprayed the entire bottle on himself that evening.

And poor Mr. Johnson was sweating like a runaway slave and tripping over his words. "No, not at all. We would never disrespect you in that way. We just want to make you and your son as comfortable as possible. Think about the boy. And how a trial and media circus would impact him."

Mr. Toole kept staring at the paper. At that point, I really doubted if he was thinking about Lester. "I want seventy-five thousand."

Mr. Johnson wiped sweat off his forehead once again while I leaned back in my chair and smiled at Mr. Toole. That son of a bitch had exposed himself and shown us his true colors. At that point, I believed that the entire story was a lie after all.

Of course, I wasn't one hundred percent certain whether or not James had molested Lester. You know I had my own reservations about James working with those kids. But I do believe that a person is innocent until proven guilty. I thought there should be a trial instead of a settlement, but seeing how Mr. Toole reacted over the money, going to trial would have been bad for both James and the school. Mr. Toole was a liar and I could now see straight through him.

"Let's not be unreasonable, Mr. Toole," Mr. Johnson said. "We're trying to be fair here."

"Seventy-five thousand or I'm out of here," he pushed. "And I will go forward with the case and do everything in my power to let everyone know what kind of school y'all really running around here."

I leaned forward and stared at him intently. My underarms were fresh with perspiration, but I kept a cool and level head and said, "Sixty thousand, and that's a final offer. Take it or leave it."

Mr. Toole extended his hand across the desk. "That sounds good to me," he said. We shook on the deal.

Mr. Johnson stood up and shook hands with Mr. Toole, too. The principal had a huge smile of relief, but Mr. Toole kept a straight face. "I'm glad we were able to work things out," said Mr. Johnson.

Mr. Toole suddenly raised his hand in the air. "Wait, before we all get ahead of ourselves."

"What is it?" asked Mr. Johnson. That grin on his face quickly disappeared. "I thought we were all clear."

"I want that faggot removed from the school," Mr. Toole said, staring at me like I had the authority to fire James.

"Watch your language, Mr. Toole," Mr. Johnson warned him. Mr. Toole had no idea that Mr. Johnson was gay himself, and I suspected he didn't give a damn either. "Let's keep this professional."

"I don't want that freak anywhere near my son," Mr. Toole insisted.

"What if we moved your son across the hall to Ms. Swaign's class?" I suggested, because firing James was completely out of the question. We would only be looking at another potential lawsuit. Although Diane had suggested that we offer James a settlement to persuade him to leave as well, I wasn't certain about that idea. My plan was to wait a couple of months for things to cool down and then lay him off along with several other teachers and staff who I had been trying to get rid of anyway. It would look totally aboveboard and no one would suspect a thing. In the end, the firm agreed with me on the handling of James.

"Well, I guess if my son won't be anywhere around him then that might work." Mr. Toole finally stretched his legs, standing in front of my desk and staring at the small piece of paper once again.

Mr. Johnson patted Mr. Toole on his back as we both walked him out the door. "You're making the right decision."

We entered the front office and immediately walked into a firestorm. James and his entourage—a tall man dressed like a woman and a real woman who looked like someone had pissed her off—were sitting and waiting.

"Is that the bastard who put his hands on you?" the woman asked. She stood up and started approaching us.

"Yeah, that's him," James said. He was egging this woman on and she was not backing down either.

She stood in front of Mr. Toole, pointing her finger in his face. "You got a lot of motherfucking nerve putting your hands on my child!"

"Woman, I don't know who you are," Mr. Toole said. "But you better get your hands out of my damn face."

"Everybody, please," Mr. Johnson interjected. As for me, I was speechless. This was something you expect to see on an episode of *Jerry Springer*, not at James Baldwin Academy. Thank God school had been dismissed for the day and it was late in the evening. "Let's just calm down."

"Calm down, my ass!" shouted the woman. James and his drag-queen friend tried to restrain her.

Anyway, between the yelling woman and the drag queen, this entire scene would have been laughable under any other circumstances. All of it was a bit overwhelming. For a minute, I couldn't even move. Their behavior was shocking to say the least.

"You guys, let's keep this professional," I said.

"Professional, my ass! Was he being professional when he put his hands on my damn son?" asked the woman. She had a mouth on her and an attitude that was out of this world. "You must don't know where we from. I'll clean the floor with your motherfucking ass."

"Come on, Ms. Flo," the drag queen said. He appeared to be the most rational one in the group. "He ain't even worth it, girl."

Mr. Toole's entire face was turning red. He was really trying hard to contain his anger, but the woman was not making it easy for him. She wanted a fight and was determined to have one.

"Let me tell you somethin'," the woman said. She had a strong presence and one of those voices that demanded respect. We all couldn't help but listen to her, even Mr. Toole. "I've dealt with people like you who think they can go around bullying everyone. But not my son, 'cause that's my child. You understand? And I don't care what you or anybody thinks of him. He's mine. And you will not disrespect him. You understand me?"

"What I understand is that you better get your hand out of my face," Mr. Toole responded. He finally had had enough. However, the woman held her ground and didn't flinch.

"James, why don't you and your friends wait inside my

office?" I finally broke my silence, trying to head off a potential disaster. But no one was listening to me or Mr. Johnson.

"I think that's a good idea," said Mr. Johnson. "Before things get out of hand."

"I ain't going nowhere until he understands where I'm coming from," the woman said, standing with both hands on her hips and staring Mr. Toole's directly in his face.

"Man, enough of this shit," Mr. Toole said, pushing the woman out of the way and escalating the situation to whole other level. "Get the hell out of my face, woman."

"Don't be pushing my mama!" James suddenly jumped in between Mr. Toole and the woman. "You must have lost your motherfucking mind!"

"Mr. Toole!" shouted Mr. Johnson. Everything was happening so fast. Mr. Toole grabbed James around his neck, choking him. And the woman reached inside her purse and pulled out a long butcher knife. My God. You could only imagine the look on my face. These people were completely out of control.

Mr. Johnson ran back inside of my office. I assumed he was calling the police, at least I hoped he was. I held my hand over my mouth in total disbelief.

"You faggot!" Mr. Toole slammed James against Ms. Edith's desk, knocking over the telephone and some important papers.

The drag queen restrained the woman, as she was about to put that long knife into Mr. Toole's back. "No, Ms. Flo, don't do it!" he shouted, taking the knife out of the woman's hand and holding her around the waist.

"Let go of me!" she yelled as Mr. Toole continued to manhandle James. He still had James around the neck, pinned down on Ms. Edith's desk. "Nobody puts their hands on my son!"

"Dad, don't!" shouted Lester. He was accompanied by Ms. Edith. I had almost forgotten that she had taken the boy upstairs to retrieve some items from James's classroom. "Let go of him!"

Poor Lester was shouting and crying. Just beside himself with grief. And he revealed something to all of us that stopped the show and brought everything to an immediate halt like the final act on Broadway. "Let him go, Dad! He didn't do nothin'! You made me say it, but he didn't even do nothin'!"

"What a day!" Mr. Johnson said on his way out of my office. He was heading home after our eventful evening. We took a moment to reflect. "Never a dull moment running a school."

"I feel sorry for Lester," I said with sadness. "What he must be going through at home."

Lester's confession was that big of a surprise to me. He was a good kid who had been forced to lie by a no-good father. Maybe Mr. Toole hated gays or he was after money all along. But either way, the man was going down.

If you could believe it, Mr. Toole actually slapped Lester out of anger for telling us the truth. Good thing the police showed up—Mr. Johnson did call them—and they took Mr. Toole in for questioning after hearing what had happened. There was suspicion of child abuse. My heart really went out to Lester for having a father like Mr. Toole, but so many of our kids were in similar circumstances. I was reminded of this every single day dealing with the students at Baldwin Academy. Poor kids today are up against so much in their young lives.

"Take it easy," Mr. Johnson. "And try not to worry. I'm sure Lester will be okay."

"I hope so, Mr. Johnson," I said. "See you tomorrow."

Afterward, I simply sat there behind my desk and exhaled. There was a stack of teacher evaluations on my desk that needed to be entered into the computer, but it wasn't going to get done that evening. I wanted to go home and take a long, hot bath. Try to forget about work, the school, Lester, James, etc.

"I'm glad you're still here," said James. He gave me an immediate headache. I thought James was long gone–him, the drag queen, and that unbelievable woman.

"I'm heading home for the evening." I stood up and grabbed my briefcase to leave. "Whatever you need to talk to me about will have to wait until the morning. I don't have time for any more drama."

"I'm by myself. I came back 'cause Johnny left a message for me on my phone," James sounded nervous. His voice was trembling. I could tell he was really upset about something.

"And what does that have to do with me?" I asked. After the awful day I had, the last thing I wanted or needed was to have a conversation about Johnny, especially with the likes of James. "I don't want to have anything to do with this."

"Listen to me," James insisted. He blocked me from going

out the door. "I think he's in trouble. On the message, he said something about Reggie and the frat finding out about him. And that they were taking him somewhere. His message got cut short, but he sounded really scared. Isn't Reggie your cousin?"

"Are you certain he said 'Reggie'?" I asked. My stomach was suddenly in knots. The last thing I wanted was for my cousin to be caught up in some mess. His frat had been known for hazing folks, and sometimes Reggie and his brothers took things too far. I had actually seen students suspended from college for hazing, and I was looking forward to seeing Reggie graduate from Wheatley, so I didn't want to see him caught up in anything like that.

"I'm positive," James said. He saw the worried expression on my face and became even more concerned. "He's really in some kind of trouble, huh?"

"Are you sure we're going in the right direction?" James asked. We were in my Range Rover heading to Rockville, Maryland, to a secluded place in the middle of nowhere. There was nothing but trees surrounding us on both sides of the highway. And it was dark, too. "We've been driving down this road for a while now."

"I'm sure this is where it is," I said to him. Apparently, Gamma Phi had selected their spring line, and Johnny was taken from campus by several members of the frat. I had made a few calls to several associates on campus and gotten an address from an old friend of a secret cabin in the woods where they initiated new members. "My friend was very thorough with his directions."

"I want to apologize for earlier," said James. "About the way we acted. My mama was just so worried about me. She wasn't thinking straight."

I clutched the steering wheel and tried to keep my eyes on the road. James and I were playing nice with each other—a far cry from our past conversations.

"Look, it's over and done with," I said. "I'm glad that your name is going to be cleared of this mess. No matter what you think of me, I wasn't hoping for you to go to jail on false accusations."

"Thank you," he said. "I appreciate that."

"I think this is it." I pulled off the road into a long driveway. The driveway led to a cabin in the woods, as I'd been told.

"I don't think any pledging is going on up here," James said, stepping out of the car and looking around outside the cabin. It was dark and totally abandoned, but I came prepared. I had two flashlights. My dad always told me to be prepared in case something happened to me on the road. Most men are surprised to find out that I can even change a tire, too. Being Dad's only child and a girl, he sometimes tried to turn me into a tomboy growing up. However, some of his advice would pay off when I was least expecting it.

"But my friend said this is where they come," I said, peeping in the window of the cabin, using my flashlight. It looked empty. There was hardly any furniture–just huge windows and darkness everywhere.

"Well, your friend obviously gave you bad information," James said, searching the area with the other flashlight. He was slowly returning to his old ways with me. I knew the nice-guy routine wouldn't last forever. "I don't have time for this."

"And you think I do?" I asked with an attitude. "To be out here with you in the middle of nowhere."

"Wait, I think I heard something," James said, walking behind the cabin. But I wasn't convinced. All I heard were the sounds of crickets and bugs and God knows what else out there in those woods. I was beginning to think this wasn't such a good idea.

"Let's just get out of here," I said, walking behind James. He was leading us to a trail behind the cabin.

"Oh, my God! Oh, my God!" James started screaming and completely freaking me out. He dropped the flashlight and was totally beside himself with shock.

"What is it?" I asked from behind him, shaking and trembling. Maybe it was the darkness or the weird sounds coming from the trees, but I can't ever recall a time when I was so terrified. "What did you see?"

James was blocking my view, but somehow the flashlight caught a glimpse of a tree with a body attached to it and I suddenly started screaming, too. "Lord God! What is this?"

What James and I saw out there in those woods that night would haunt us forever. It was the most sadistic and twisted thing I have ever seen in my life. All I remember was the large amount of blood running down his legs.

"Oh, my God! Johnny!" shouted James. He was down on his knees beside the tree. "What have they done to you?"

14

Johnny

"Is my son going to be all right, Doctor?" Mom's voice was the first one I heard coming out of what felt like a deep sleep. She was crying, man, and I hated to see Moms hurting for any reason. And I noticed my pops, too. They were talking to this black dude in a long white coat. All of them looked like a blur to me. Something was wrong with my vision and that freaked me out big-time.

"Moms." I struggled to get a few simple words out of my mouth. It was painful for me to even talk, man. In fact, my whole body felt like someone had crushed me underneath a car. "Why are you crying?"

"Thank the good Lord," Moms sat in a chair next to the bed and immediately started rubbing the top of my forehead. "You're up. I'm so glad to hear your beautiful voice."

I tried to raise my right hand to wipe those tears from Moms's eyes, but noticed that my arm was in a cast—both of them. I felt something wrapped around my head. Panic began to sink in. "Where am I?"

"Son, you're in the hospital," said Pops. He was standing over Moms—both him and the black dude—as she continued to stroke my forehead. "But you're going to be all right."

"How you feeling, Johnny?" the black dude asked. He must have seen the frown on my face and quickly introduced himself. "I'm Dr. McLawson and you're in Rockville Medical Center. Do you feel any pain?"

"A little," I moaned. I tried to move my legs, but couldn't. Both my legs were in casts, too. Man, I was beat up really badly, and it didn't take a doctor to tell me that—pain was moving through my body like a bolt of electricity. "What happened?"

"You don't remember, son?" asked Pops.

I stared at Dr. McLawson—all of us did. He stood over me and checked my vision with a small white light.

"It's not uncommon for someone who's experienced trauma to the head," Dr. McLawson explained, "to have some trouble remembering things in the immediate present."

"Can the memory loss be permanent?" asked Moms. She looked as horrible as I felt.

One thing about my Moms, man, was that she was a real positive, spiritual woman, and it took a lot to rattle her cage. Being the first lady of a black church, you have to be grounded. She had to be, with Pops being the pastor of a large congregation and having people pull at him from every direction. The church expected a lot from their pastor and first lady. I can't tell you how many funerals they attended, how many sickbeds of affliction they prayed over.

Moms was strong and the backbone of everything, though. She would keep Pops going when he got down and tired of the hustle and bustle of being a pastor. But, you know, everyone has a breaking point. Man, me being up in that hospital bed and looking the way I did may have been Moms's. Although my peeps had seen just about everything, too, nothing prepared them for seeing their own blood in that situation—their youngest son on his deathbed.

"Let's not panic or get ahead of ourselves," said Dr. McLawson. He was the calm voice that was definitely needed. "The CAT scan didn't show any reason for concern. Johnny, who's the President of the United States?"

"George W. Bush," I said with confidence. Pops hugged Moms. I imagined they were both relieved to know that I hadn't completely lost my memory.

"And what year is it?" the doctor continued.

"Two thousand six."

"Good." Dr. McLawson wrote something in my medical chart and placed it in a slot beside the bed. "You've been through quite an ordeal, but from what your parents tell me, you're a fighter."

"What about his legs and arms?" Moms asked, taking the words out of my mouth.

"There was major damage to bone and tissues," the doctor said, "but we've taken care of most of the problems during surgery. The good news is that the X-rays didn't reveal any severe damage to internal organs, which is what we were originally concerned about."

"Thank you, Lord," Moms said, squeezing Pops's hand. The both of them were in tears. Man, I can't ever recall seeing Pops cry either, so I know this had to be hard on him, too.

"Right now, our patient needs a lot of rest," Dr. McLawson said. "So not too many visitors at one time, and let's keep the visits short. It's going to take some time, but I'm optimistic that he will make a full recovery and regain the use of his arms and legs."

"Doc, my eyes hurt," I said. "Everything seems a little blurry."

"I wouldn't be too concerned about that," he said. "You've been given a lot of medication, and you took a hit to the head and there was some swelling, but once it heals you'll regain your full vision as well. We took real good care of you."

"Somebody hit me in the head?" I asked with a confused look on my face. "Who would do something like that to me?"

"Sweetheart, don't worry about that," Moms said. "Just focus on your recovery."

"She's right, son," Pops jumped in with his two cents. Man, at that point I felt like they were keeping something from me and that made me more upset than anything.

"What are ya'll not telling me, man?" I asked. "Who did this to me?"

"Where's my handsome grandson?" Grandma Eve said as she came through the door. She was in a wheelchair—Carl was pushing her around. Tiffany was behind them. "I knew dat you was gone be just fine. I told 'em dat you were strong as a nail."

"Grandma," I said, and smiled as she held her wrinkled hands up against my cheek. Man, seeing my grandma's face and smile took my mind off of everything; at least for the moment, anyway. "I was wondering where you were."

"I've been here the whole time," she said, flashing her white teeth. Grandma Eve lit up a room with her smile, man. She was like a good hymn on a Sunday morning. Her hand felt warm up against my cheekbone, too. "They will all tell you."

"Glad to see you up and talking, my brother," Carl said. "You had us all worried there for a minute."

"I second that motion," said Tiffany. "We love you and have been praying for your recovery."

"Well, y'all ain't gone get rid of me that easy," I said, looking around at all of them. Their faces staring down at me in that bed gave me a warm feeling. I saw nothing but love inside of them, man, and that was the best gift in the world. But still there was one face missing. I was wondering where James was. Why wasn't he there with my family? Then, it dawned on me how bad things had been between us. James was probably staying away to keep the peace, as least that was what I was thinking at the time.

"I plan to be around for a long time," I continued.

"Well, I think I'll give you some family time alone," said Dr. McLawson. He was preparing to leave, but Pops quickly stopped him.

"I want you to stay for a minute," Pops said, picking up a

Bible from the nightstand beside my bed. "We have a lot to be thankful for and we owe much of it to you and this hospital for taking good care of our son."

"Oh, I'm just doing my job," said Dr. McLawson, "but thanks anyway."

"And a fine job you did, too, Doctor," Grandma Eve said. "We all appreciate you. We is a praying family, Doctor. And I think what my son is trying to say is, will you stay and have a word of prayer with us?"

"Of course I will," he said. "I recognize that I wouldn't be able to do anything without the man upstairs. He's the one who really does the healing."

"Why don't we all take a hand and form a circle around his bed," Moms said. They formed what Pops called a Holy Ghost circle around me. When I was little I used to accompany Pops to visit church members who were sick in the hospital. So you could imagine I had seen a lot of these Holy Ghost circles in my lifetime.

"Bow your heads," said Pops. He now had his glasses on and the Bible opened. "Let us pray. Heavenly Father, we humbly come to you with thanksgiving in our hearts, Father God, thanking you for yet another day to come together in prayer."

As Pops prayed, I had my eyes closed and I began to lose hold of his voice. I was slipping further and deeper into the darkness. And in this dark place there was no God: nothing but pure evilness and hatred . . .

"You know what you are!" I heard a voice shout from the

corner of the room. I was sitting in a chair with both my arms tied behind my back. There was something over my head– maybe a sheet. I don't know. But I could hear voices in my head. And they were mad voices. Evil voices. Angry and loud. "A stinking faggot!"

Someone sent a fist up against my head. And then that fist was followed by more fists. They were punching me from the right and the left, from the front and the back. I felt like a train wreck. My head was spinning and hurting.

"Please God!" I was screaming. "Don't do this, man!"

"Shut up, you fucking faggot!" someone said. But that voice I recognized. It was Reggie. I couldn't believe this. If anyone, I would have suspected Rafer–not my homeboy who had been looking out for me from the beginning. This was twisted, man. "Ain't no God coming to help you!"

"Reggie, is that you, man?" I asked. The voices suddenly got quiet. They had been exposed. I could actually hear them breathing. "I know that's you, man. Don't do this. I'm sorry for everything."

"Untie him," said Reggie. I thought I was finally getting through to him. My heart was pumping with excitement and fear at the same time. Maybe Reggie was there to actually save me, I thought to myself.

"Why?" someone asked.

"Just do it," Reggie said. He seemed to be on my side until I heard those final words that changed everything. "Untie him and drag his ass outside."

"What you doing, man?" I asked as they pulled me out of the chair by both of my legs and dragged me across the cold wooden floor. I was grabbing for something to hold on to, but there was nothing in my path. I had no idea where I was. I was terrified.

Reggie continued to give instructions. "Tie him to the tree." I was trying to fight, man. I was screaming and kicking, but there were too many of them. I was down on the ground and they were punching and kicking me all in my ass. They started jumping on top of my back. They jumped on my arms and legs. I felt my bones breaking, crackling like wood in a fireplace.

"Please, man!" I screamed. Somebody took me around my neck and lifted me off the ground.

"Shut the hell up!" Reggie screamed. "You brought this on yourself. I told you that this frat was not for your kind. I took you in and befriended you. You lied to me!"

"I'm sorry, man," I cried like a bitch. They were tying me to the tree with my face pressed against the trunk. I heard the birds chirping in my head. "I'm so sorry. I didn't mean it."

"Take down his pants," I heard Reggie say.

"What for?" someone questioned him. "I don't wanna see that faggot's ass."

"Move," Reggie said. "I'll do it myself."

He pulled down my pants and my ass was wide open and exposed. I felt the coldness against my butt.

"Hand me the paddle," said Reggie. I immediately started yelling when I realized what he had in store for me. Reggie was about to paddle me on my bare ass. They had paddled me before with my clothes on during the pre-initiation process, and that shit was painful. I already knew what to expect, and it was going to be excruciating.

"Stop, man!" I begged for Reggie's mercy as the paddle hit my ass. It left my butt cheeks stinging, and I was going into shock, shaking and trembling with my face pressed against the tree.

Suddenly, everyone was paddling me and cursing my name. They paddled me for so long that after a while my ass felt numb. I couldn't even feel the pain. And I was exhausted and dizzy. My butt felt like it had been split wide open, and I could actually feel blood running down my legs. It was the blood. It was the blood that scared them.

"Let's get the hell out of here, man!"

I called out for help, but nobody heard me. I heard the birds chirping in my head. Tears ran down my face, soaking through the sheet still over my head. I was passing out, slipping in and out of darkness. I couldn't tell if it was night or day. All I remember was falling into a deep, deep darkness.

"Let the people of God say 'Amen.'" I got hold of my Pops's voice again. It was leading me out of the darkness. But I couldn't see. My eyes were opened, but I couldn't see anything, man. At that point, I didn't know if I was still tied to the tree or inside the hospital room. I was screaming and going crazy.

"Sweetheart, calm down," Moms said. Her voice was loud and ringing in my ears. "Before you hurt yourself."

I was screaming and trying to get out of the bed.

"Son, what's wrong?" asked Pops. "Doctor!"

I suddenly felt a needle in my shoulder. It stung against my bare skin. I was slowly slipping back into the darkness.

"You gone be all right, Johnny," Grandma Eve said. It felt like I was now floating to heaven. And for some reason I believed what she was saying to me. Her sweet voice put me to sleep. "Don't worry about nothin' 'cause Grandma right here by your side. And you gone be just fine, my sweetheart. Just fine."

"About time you get your ass up, nigga," Carl said. He was smiling down at me. There was no darkness. I could actually see him! "You got everybody fooled, but I know what kind of game you're playing."

I stared at him and smiled. Man, my brother knew he was a fool sometime. But me and Carl always had that kind of relationship where we joked around with each other.

"What you talking about, man?" I asked him, forcing a smile and frowning. The darkness may have been gone, but that pain was shooting through a nigga faster than the speed of light.

"You're trying to get out of helping with the Easter eggs," said Carl. Every Easter, Grandma Eve would have us coloring eggs with her. When we were littler that shit was fun, but now that we grown-ass men that ain't cool, man. Not at all. Me, Carl, and Ronnie, my oldest brother who lives in Texas, laugh about it every year. In fact, the entire family makes fun of us coloring Easter eggs with Grandma Eve. But that's our grandma, man, and it's those little things that make her happy. We do it for her well-being, but still a nigga be trying to get out of it every Easter.

"Man, you're crazy," I said. "You better get your apron ready, fool. You know she say you make the best ones."

Carl laughed. "That's cold, man. But it's all good. Easter is two months away and she's already talking about it."

"Where's everybody?"

"Mom and Pop took Grandma home," he said, "and Tiffany went down to the cafeteria for something to eat."

I suddenly got quiet on Carl, thinking about James. He was on my mind a lot. I needed him there with me.

"What's wrong with you?" asked Carl. He was smiling and being playful. "Getting all quiet on a nigga?"

"Have you seen James?" I asked. He wiped that smile off his face. It was no secret that Carl couldn't stand James for nothing in the world, man. James was too much of a reminder that his little brother was gay.

You see, Carl was still holding on to the straight Johnny who grew up with him playing football and chasing young girls. I'm still that Johnny minus the chasing girls. I have the same heart and soul, but for some reason Carl couldn't get with my lifestyle. Where most of the family had accepted me, Carl had put up the most resistance.

"He's outside," said Carl. "Been here the whole time."

"Then why didn't he come in?" I looked puzzled.

"'Cause you heard the doctor, nigga," Carl said with an attitude. I could tell he wasn't feeling the idea of me asking him about James. "Not too many visitors at one time."

"Could you get him for me?" I asked. Carl hesitated for a moment. I imagined this was hard for him.

"Sure, if that's what you want, my brother," he said. "I'll be right outside if you need me."

"Thanks, man," I said, staring him in the eyes. No doubt, me and Carl had a lot of love for each other even though we couldn't see eye to eye on the gay thing.

"Look at you," James said, entering the room and trying to soften the mood. But he had tears in his eyes. He was crying. James had a hard time with hospital rooms and funerals. He had lost a lot of friends to AIDS and gotten sick of seeing death. "You look almost as bad as I did a couple of years ago."

"I see you got jokes," I said. He was referring to that incident when my cousin Kojack shot him and left him for dead. But time heals all wounds. I never thought we would get to the point where we could joke about something like that, especially under the current circumstances.

James sat in the chair next to the bed with a purse on his shoulders—he always had that purse, you know—and stared at me real hard. One look in his eyes and I could see he still had much love for me. I noticed he had dried-up mud on his clothes, which was totally unlike James. He was a neat freak and cared a whole lot about how he looked.

"You look a mess," I said. "I know I got an excuse. But what's yours?"

"It's a long story," he said, sitting his purse beside the bed. "I'll tell you about it later. Right now I'm worried about you. How you feeling?"

"Well, I guess okay," I said. "Considering everything is broken on my body."

"You mean everything?" James asked real suggestively. He was being silly and playful. "At least I hope not."

"Oh, don't worry about that part of the body," I said. "Believe me. It's still very much functional."

"That's good to know," he said. Man, I couldn't believe this shit, but he had my dick rising. Here I was in a hospital bed with broken legs and arms and my dick was getting hard. I could no longer fight the feeling. James got under my skin and that was all there was to it, man.

He was laughing and crying at the same time. "I've been so worried about you. Your family wouldn't let me come in."

"Come on now, man," I said. "Don't start that crying on me. Between you, my mama, and my grandma y'all gone have my ass swimming in a river. I must look real bad, huh?"

James got quiet. He didn't want me to know just how bad it was.

"Is it that bad?" I asked. "Let me see. I know you got a mirror in that purse."

"Hon, let's not worry about that," he said. "Let's focus on the positive. I heard you gone make a full recovery. That's great."

"Don't change the subject," I said. "Hold the mirror in front of me."

At first, James was resistant, but he eventually reached inside his purse and slowly held the mirror to my face.

"Honey, don't worry about it," James said to try to comfort me. I was shaking my head in disbelief. Man, I didn't even recognize myself. My face was completely distorted. "It's going to heal and you'll look like your old self again in no time."

I dropped my head on the pillow with tears rolling down my cheeks. What kind of animals would do something like this to another human being, man? What kind of animals? That was the question that had me crying. I was crying for me and them. Man, I was weeping from the deep pit of my gut.

"Come on, Johnny. Don't do this to me," James said. He had never seen me like this before. It must have scared him. "We gone get through this together like everything else."

15

James

"After everything my boy did for Johnny, I can't believe y'all gone keep him from going inside that room," said Flo. She was standing up for me against Johnny's parents, who were doing everything in their power to keep me and him apart. Mr. and Mrs. Lomack were guarding Johnny's hospital room like pit bulls. "And y'all call yourselves Christians."

We were in some hospital in Rockville, Maryland. I couldn't believe that Johnny had been brutally attacked by members of that fraternity he wanted to pledge. I knew in my gut them motherfuckers weren't no good for Johnny. When I heard how they had treated Kevin, I knew that brotherhood shit was about nothing but talk. Gamma Phi was no more than a bunch of lowlife hoodlums who deserved to be in jail, 'cause it was a crying shame how they beat Johnny and left him for dead. And now all I wanted to do was be there for Johnny—by his side—

but loving him always seemed to be a fight and struggle, especially when it came to his overprotective family.

"Our son needs his rest," Mrs. Lomack said in a low voice. She sounded tired and looked weak. Mrs. Lomack had her hair pulled back in a ponytail and wasn't wearing any makeup, which was totally unlike her.

Let me say, Johnny's mama is a diva, honey. It's very rare to catch that girl without makeup or a fresh hairdo. What I'm really trying to say was that this situation with Johnny was hard on Mrs. Lomack and everybody who loved him, which was one of the reasons why me and Flo couldn't understand why they were treating me like the devil. Shit, I wasn't the enemy. I was grieving for Johnny, too.

"I'm not going to bother Johnny," I said. "I just wanna sit with him for a while."

"You already had a visit with him, son," Mr. Lomack said without apology. I noticed large bags under his eyes. "You can come back tomorrow and maybe you can visit with him at that time."

"Chile, let's go," Flo said as she took me by the arm. I pulled away. There was no way I was leaving Johnny's side. "I told you, you should never have moved up here in the first place. These people don't give a damn about you. Can't you see that?"

"This isn't personal," said Mr. Lomack. He held his wife close to him. "We are just worried about our son."

"My boy is the one who found your son!" Flo shouted in his face. That girl was getting to a boiling point and I was beginning to worry, y'all. When Flo started boiling, anything was bound to happen.

You don't have to take my word for it. Ask Mr. Toole. Flo went after his lying ass with a knife inside of Sheila's office, honey. Thank God Mookie was there to stop her. Things could have gotten a lot uglier. Although Mr. Toole would have deserved to have a knife in his back—for lying on me—I wasn't trying to see my mama going to nobody's jail over stupid shit. You feel me? There's always a silver lining behind a dark cloud though. Lester told the truth, honey. Told everybody that his daddy made him lie against me. Case closed.

"If it wasn't for Johnny," continued Flo. She was getting loud up in that hospital. There were a few people staring at us in the corridor. But ask me if Flo gave a damn. Hell no. I kept my cool though as long as Flo didn't pull out a butcher knife on those people, honey, like she did with Mr. Toole. "Your precious son would be dead. Probably would have bled to death. So, you should be thanking my boy instead of trying to hate on him."

Flo was partly right, 'cause it was me *and Sheila* who found Johnny in those woods. We found him in the woods tied to a damn tree like a slave. The only thing that was missing was a noose around his neck. And it was Sheila's crazy, homophobic-ass cousin who led this assault against Johnny. Although I didn't blame her personally, I still held Ms. Girl responsible in a way.

Part of me wondered if she had anything to do with her cousin being so angry with Johnny in the first place. You know,

I just wasn't trusting anybody when it came to this crime. 'Cause after what I had been through with Mr. Toole accusing me of molesting his son, I knew firsthand how cruel people can be. No matter how good you are out here in this world, folks still gone do you wrong. Period.

"You and Johnny have both been through so much," Mrs. Lomack said. She was staring at me so hard that it gave me the chills. It was the same look that I had gotten many times from Bible-toting folks who believed they were doing the will of God. "It was only a couple of years ago you were fighting for your own life. Maybe God is speaking something to the both of you about the way you've been living."

"So let me get this right," I said with a grin on my face. That was the only way I could restrain myself. Mrs. Lomack had completely fallen off her rocker. "The reason why Kojack shot me and some thugs almost killed your son is because God hates us for being gay? Is that what you really think?"

Mrs. Lomack stared at me and then Flo with shame. She had a look of regret on her face, too. Her eyes began to water. "I don't know what I'm saying. I'm just so worried about my son."

Mrs. Lomack suddenly fell inside of her husband's arms, weeping. She was crying on his shoulder, uncontrollably. Of course I felt sorry for the woman. That was the only reason why I wasn't giving her a piece of my mind for that ignorant-ass comment about God hating on me and Johnny 'cause of our sexuality.

"And just when I thought I had heard it all," Flo said, pulling a cigarette out of her purse and staring in my direction. "Chile, I'm going smoke me a cigarette to calm my nerves. Are you gone be all right?"

I nodded. "I'm good. I'll be right here when you get back. Believe me. I ain't going anywhere soon."

Flo took off and left the three of us standing there in the corridor. I was glad Flo was somewhere smoking her cigarette, honey. For one, it kept that girl calm and under control. Besides, this wasn't her battle to fight. If I wanted a future with Johnny, I had to deal with his parents one way or the other.

"Look, I'm not trying to cause any trouble," I said to both of them. "I'm worried about Johnny, too."

Mrs. Lomack continued to weep in her husband's arms.

"Son, this isn't the time," Mr. Lomack said, rubbing his wife's back. "Please come back tomorrow."

"Is everything all right over here?" A slender white police officer glided up behind us and asked. "Ma'am, are you okay?"

Mrs. Lomack stared at the police officer, pulling a handkerchief out of her purse. She wiped her nose. "I'm fine, officer. You must be here to take my son's statement?"

"Is this a good time?" asked the officer. He was very polite and respectful. The reason this stood out to me was because most of them police officers are no good, honey. And one thing they can't stand is a black man—gay, straight, or whatever. If you don't believe me, go on a road trip with me and let us get stopped by a white police officer. Honey, you be lucky if you don't get your ass beat down like Rodney King. "I can come back another time if it isn't."

"That won't be necessary." Mr. Lomack opened Johnny's door for the officer. "My son has been waiting to give his statement."

Mrs. Lomack followed the police officer into the room.

"Please give us this time," Mr. Lomack turned to me and said. This man wouldn't quit. Here his son was in that room probably going over details of the worst experience in his life and Mr. Lomack was more preoccupied with keeping me away from him. "If not for me, do it for Johnny, son."

"Whatever." I finally gave up. I walked away from the door and took a seat in the lobby of the hospital. Sometimes you have to choose your battles. Fighting Johnny's parents when he was already dealing with so much would not have been a smart move on my part. In the end, I would have looked like the bad guy.

"Is someone sitting here, ma'am?" I asked an elderly lady with a breathing mask over her face. She had an oxygen tank beside her. That girl didn't look good at all.

She removed the breathing mask. Her voice sounded weird, like she had something caught in her throat. "No, you can sit there."

So I did, trying not to stare at the woman, but she was one of the reasons why I hated hospitals, honey. From the pale white walls to the sick patients to the long, dreary corridors, I suddenly felt ill myself waiting inside that hospital to see my Johnny. The entire place gave me the creeps and made my skin crawl.

I looked up from a magazine just in the nick of time. Kevin

was pushing through the lobby, heading to Johnny's room. "Kevin, over here."

"What's up, baby?" Kevin said, hugging me tightly. I noticed a bag inside his hand. "How's Johnny?"

"He's getting better," I said, "but it's gonna be a long and slow recovery. What's in the bag?"

Kevin took out a pair of jeans and a stylish T-shirt with Beyoncé on the front. He knew I was a big fan of hers. Back in the day, when I was performing in gay clubs and doing drag, Beyoncé was my diva of choice. "Since you won't leave this hospital, I brought something for you to wear."

"Hon, I can't believe you did this for me," I said, staring at him with tears in my eyes. Kevin was such a nice guy and so thoughtful, too. You know, his kindness touched my heart.

"Well, I couldn't let you keep what you had on," he said, handing the bag over to me. "Have you looked in the mirror lately?"

I looked myself over and shook my head. There was dry mud at the bottom of my jeans. "I do look a mess, but Reggie looks worse."

After I found Johnny in those woods and saw how badly he was hurt, I completely lost it, y'all. Once me and Sheila got him to the hospital, I called Kevin and had him take me up to Wheatley College. I made him take me up there to find that dude Reggie. I was gone beat Reggie's black ass, y'all. I was gone beat his ass old-school style with my bare fist. But God must have been on his side, 'cause we searched that entire campus for Reggie and couldn't locate him.

After searching for over an hour, me and Kevin were about to give up. And then we found Reggie's silver Mercedes-Benz with Gamma Phi license plate parked on campus. Kevin recognized the car. Apparently that bastard came from money. Both Reggie's parents were big-shot business execs up in New York. All the money in the world couldn't save his ass though.

I took an iron rod that I had found near the Dumpster and started breaking his windows. I broke out his windows and then busted his tires. It was raining, muddy, and slippery, but somehow I managed to get the job done. By the time I was finished, Reggie's beautiful Mercedes looked like something from a junkyard sale.

"I still can't believe you did that to the dude's car," Kevin said.

"Well, he deserved it," I said. "But that's a car. He can get another one. Johnny, on the other hand, could have been killed."

"You're right about that," he said. "You definitely can't compare the two."

"But, anyway, I know I must smell like a can of fish, huh?" I said jokingly, trying to lighten the mood.

"You would have to have a pussy to smell like fish," he said, "and from what I heard you don't got one of those."

"How you know what I got?" I asked, being playful with him. It was fun flirting with Kevin. He was such an easy target. You know, I sensed on some level he liked me in that way. "You ain't never been down there to see."

"And you're right about that," Kevin said with a grin on his face. "I can't even touch that one."

I placed the pair of jeans and T-shirt back in the bag. "Where's Mookie?"

Kevin suddenly got quiet on me. There was a strange look on his face. "He hasn't called you?"

"Not since the other day when Johnny was checked into the hospital," I said. "Why? Something wrong?"

"He's probably going to kill me for telling you this," Kevin said. "You know how private he can be."

I was already thinking the worst. Mookie had been looking sick for weeks, losing weight and not eating. The big "A" word was in the back of my head. I couldn't believe I was about to go through this again. So many friends of mine had died of AIDS. "Tell me. What's up with Mookie?"

"He's sick," Kevin said. "He's really sick."

"I knew something was wrong," I said. "He has AIDS, huh?"

Kevin frowned. "No, he doesn't have AIDS. What made you think that?"

"The weight loss," I said, "not eating."

"Well, I can see how you got that idea," said Kevin. "Mookie has a sickness, but it's not AIDS. Mookie is suffering from anorexia. And you really need to go see him. It's that bad."

"Hon, get your ass up out of that bed," I said to Mookie upon entering his bedroom. He was lying underneath the covers. When I pulled the sheets off of him, I wanted to cry. Poor Mookie looked so frail and weak. He had always been skinny, but now I could actually see his bones. And this was the first time I had seen him with all of his clothes off. It was really scary how much weight he had lost. "'Cause I'm taking your ass to the hospital. Kevin told me everything."

"Leave me alone," Mookie moaned. He held on to his pillow. "I'm not going no damn hospital. And what are you doing here, anyway? I thought you were with Johnny."

"Johnny is going to be fine," I said to him, digging in his closet for clothes. Mookie had been a good friend to me since I arrived in DC, and that was the only reason why I left that hospital. He was the only person who could get me to leave Johnny's side. "Right now, I'm concerned about you. I am not going to let you die. You hear me? I'm not gone do it, hon."

Once I got something in my mind, there was no stopping me. And although I had no experience dealing with someone with anorexia, I knew it was something serious and could be deadly.

I was watching *Oprah* one day and these twins had anorexia. They refused to eat because they felt fat. They were skinny as hell! Yet they felt like five-hundred-pound women, honey. It was insane. I had always thought that anorexia was something white folks went through. You know, the tall, slender white girl complex. Shit, all the black people I knew had no problem eating. I guess there was a first time for everything.

"Here, put this on." I threw a pair of jeans on the bed. Mookie still held on to the pillow like it was his savior. He really looked horrible, y'all. "You can come back with me to Rockville. They have some good doctors out there."

"Leave me alone, bitch," he said, pulling the covers back over himself. "Ain't nothing the matter with me."

"Have you seen how bad you look?" I got real with his ass. Maybe that was the problem. Nobody was giving the truth to Mookie straight up. Most of his friends were scared of him, honey. Mookie could be cold and raw. But me–I wasn't scared of him at all. "You look a hot mess. And you need to get this problem of yours taken care of."

"I need a joint," he said. "Get me a joint and I'll feel a whole lot better."

I pulled a mirror off Mookie's dresser and placed it in front of him. "Look at yourself in the mirror. This is serious. Look at yourself!"

It was like déjà vu. Only yesterday I was putting a mirror in front of Johnny so he could see what those savages had done to him. This was different though. Mookie was doing this to himself and that was what made this situation even more sad and depressing.

"I ain't gone tell you again. Get that mirror out of my face, bitch," said Mookie. He tried to knock the mirror out of my hand, but I wouldn't let him. In fact, I pulled him by the back of his head and forced the mirror in his face.

"Look at yourself!" I shouted, pulling his head toward the mirror. "You are dying 'cause you're not eating! Can't you see that?"

Mookie caught a glimpse of himself in that mirror and immediately started crying. He was crying, y'all, like an infant straight out of the womb. I had finally broken Mookie down to reality. But being the friend that I am to him, I was also right there to lift him up, too.

"It's gone be all right." I rocked Mookie in my arms like a mother tending to her child. "You've always been there for me. And I'm gone be right here for you, too. You're not alone in this fight. Believe that."

When we got back to Rockville, it was late. Mookie was quickly checked into the hospital. His situation was serious, but not fatal. Doctors expected to get him functioning and eating in no time. Mookie would probably need therapy, too. Whatever it took, I asked those doctors to make it happen. You know, I was so relieved that Mookie was finally going to get the help he needed.

"You just getting back?" asked Flo. She had been sleeping in a chair in the lobby and was now stretching her arms. "How's your friend Mookie?"

"He got checked into the hospital," I said, handing Flo a cup of coffee. My poor mama was hanging in there with me throughout this entire ordeal. And it meant a lot, too. "When they saw how skinny he was, they put him in front of everyone."

"If it ain't one thing it's another," Flo said, sipping her coffee. "Johnny's parents left a few minutes ago. He's all alone now. I stuck my head in, but he was sleeping."

Honey, you know that was all I needed to hear. With Johnny's family long gone, we could finally have some intimate time together. My plan to outlast them had worked.

"Wake up, sleepyhead," I said and took a seat next to Johnny's bed. He was coming out of a deep sleep. There were IV tubes and machines hooked to his body. It wasn't as scary as it looked. I had been there before myself. "I think you've had enough beauty rest."

Johnny cleared his throat and smiled. "I was beginning to think you ran off on me."

"Don't blame me," I said. "Your family are the ones who're tripping. You know they been blocking me from seeing you."

Johnny shook his head. "I'm sorry they're treating you like that. I'm'a have to have a talk with them about that shit."

"Anyway, how you feeling?" I carefully touched the cast on his arm. "You sound better."

"Thanks," said Johnny. He was staring at me real hard. I could tell he had something on his mind. "I've been lying here and doing a lot of thinking."

"Well, you do have a lot of time on your hands," I tried to interject a little humor. "I can only imagine what thoughts are running through that brain of yours."

Johnny kept his eyes on me, wiped that smile off his face. "What happened with you and that crazy parent at the school?"

"The truth came out," I said. "And I'm glad to put that mess behind me."

"I'm glad things worked out for you," said Johnny. He was sounding so sincere and getting so emotional that in a minute I thought he might actually break out crying again. "I know you've had a hard time of it lately. And I haven't made it any easier."

"Hon, let's not talk about." I patted his arm. Johnny was now tapping into my emotions and I wasn't interested in going there with him. You know, I was trying to stay strong. "Just focus on getting better."

"No, listen to me," Johnny pushed. The numbers on one of those machines started going up. It must have been Johnny's heart, because he was getting so emotional and upset. Only the human heart could set off that kind of reaction. "I need to talk to you."

"Calm down, hon," I said. "I'm not going anywhere. Just calm down before you set one of these machines off."

"I know I treated you like shit," Johnny continued anyway. He chose his words very carefully. "Tried to change you into somebody you weren't. I'm sorry for being an asshole."

"We both made our share of mistakes," I said, trying not to look him in the eyes. Johnny had so much pain and sorrow in his eyes that it was drowning me. "We have plenty of time to talk about all of that, hon."

"You're not listening to me, man." He coughed. His lungs sounded like garbage. "I have to tell you something."

My heart started racing, because I knew something was deeply wrong. It was the calm before the storm, and my stomach was suddenly in knots. "What's so important that it can't wait?"

Tears started falling from Johnny's eyes. I was beginning to realize that this was serious. Johnny was making a confession. "You've been by my side through this situation and so much more and I don't deserve it."

"I love you, hon," I said. "You've been there for me, too."

"I don't deserve it," said Johnny. Tears continued to flow from his eyes. "Me and Sheila—"

I immediately cut him off. "Wait a minute. This is about Sheila? What does she have to do with any of this?"

Johnny got spooky quiet on me, y'all. He became so silent that it scared me to the core. When I looked in his eyes, I knew what he was trying to tell me. It was something about the way he was staring at me. Men have a way of telling on themselves with their eyes.

"How could you?" I stood up to leave. My heart was on the floor. "You slept with Sheila, didn't you? I knew something was going on between the two of you."

"It only happened that one time," he quickly tried to explain himself. The number on one of those machines was going through the roof. "It didn't mean anything. It was a mistake."

"How is your dick falling inside of her a mistake?" I asked. "Explain that to me."

"You have every right to be upset with me," said Johnny. He had calmed himself down. "I'm upset with myself. Man, I have made so many mistakes this past year, trying to please my parents. My brother."

"Oh no, you're not going to blame this on anyone else," I said. "You did this. Not your parents or your brother. You're a selfish bastard. I can't even look at you."

For a minute, there were no words between us. I stared into his eyes and felt like something was slipping away like a ship straight out of dock. Our love was floating down the river.

"Is this a good time?" asked Sheila. I couldn't believe that she had entered the room, especially at that moment.

I turned around and stared at her. She was holding a lovely bouquet of flowers and looking totally clueless. Sheila had no idea of the firestorm she had walked in on.

"Those are beautiful," I said with a fake smile on my face.

"Thanks. I picked them up from the hospital store," she said. "How's he doing?"

"Why don't you ask him yourself." I was short and cold with her. Johnny lay in the bed with a blank look on his face. I could only imagine what he was thinking, 'cause, baby, he knows I'm my mother's son. Under different circumstances, I would have slapped Sheila's face and knocked her ass straight out of those pumps. But I kept my cool, y'all. I was really proud of myself.

"How you feeling?" Sheila walked over to Johnny's side. "I thought these might brighten up the room."

Johnny kept his eyes on me the whole time. After a while, I could no longer pretend.

"You two liars deserve each other!" I yelled. "He's all yours!"

"James, wait!" shouted Johnny. "Don't go like this!"

I walked out of the room and slammed the door on the both of them.

16

Sheila

"Reggie, why did you want to see me?" I immediately asked. We were inside a holding room in the police station. Reggie had been arrested for leading an attack on Johnny. He even had on handcuffs. This was such a shock. I had no idea that my cousin was homophobic. A few years ago there was a rumor of him being involved in a gang fight against a gay student. I never believed that Reggie was guilty. This attack on Johnny was quite telling about my cousin's true character and nature.

"I really can't help you." I was very dry and to the point with him.

"Oh, it's like that," he said with a hurt look on his face. Reggie stood directly in my face and stared me in my eyes. "I'm family and you gone treat me like this?"

"Don't you understand what you've done?" I said, placing my purse on the table. There was nothing but a table and two chairs in the room. An old black police officer was posted by the door, looking like he would rather be anywhere else but inside that room. I couldn't blame the man, as I was feeling exactly the same way. "You almost killed somebody."

"It wasn't me, cuz," said Reggie. He sounded desperate and scared. "He told the police he heard my voice, but I wasn't even there. I was with my girl. You could ask her."

"I'm not the one you need to be trying to convince," I said, taking a seat at the table. "Because the police are convinced they got the right guy."

Reggie sat across from me and placed his hands on the table. I hated seeing him in those handcuffs. This was my cousin, for heaven's sake. Reggie and I grew up together and had been close since childhood. This was not how I imagined his life turning out when we were kids. We both had such big dreams for our lives and now he had thrown everything away over such foolishness.

But isn't that the story with most of our black men? They do some of the most dumb, cruel things without thinking of the consequences. Hell, I was mad at Reggie for throwing his future away.

"I didn't do it, cuz," he insisted. "He's trying to blame it on the frat 'cause he didn't make the line. He's angry with us."

Reggie had been the only member of Gamma Phi arrested. Johnny couldn't place anyone else at the scene of the incident. He had only recognized Reggie's voice, but it was enough to convince the police. It really wasn't looking good for my cousin, but he refused to bring other members of the fraternity down with him.

"You need to cut some kind of plea bargain with the DA," I said. This was the only advice I could give Reggie, knowing what he was facing. If convicted, my cousin was looking at some serious jail time. "And tell them who else was involved. I heard you're refusing to cooperate with the investigation."

"I'll never give up the frat!" He slammed his hands on the table. "You understand. I'll die for the frat before I give them up. Fuck these people in here."

"Now you're being stupid," I said. "While you're rotting in jail, do you think the frat is going to be thinking about you?"

"Yep," he said. "'Cause those my niggas. My blood."

"I see there's just no getting through to you," I said with tears in my eyes. Reggie was in his own world and there was simply no reaching him. "This is serious."

"He had a sheet over his head," said Reggie. He was trying to defend himself. "How could he identify me if he couldn't even see me? He had a sheet over his head."

"And how do you know that, Reggie?" I asked. "If you weren't there."

He suddenly got quiet and thought about it for a moment. "That's what I heard, that he had a sheet over his head."

"I don't believe you," I said. "You even look guilty."

"What happened to innocent until proven guilty?" he asked.

"That's up to the court to decide, but I know what I saw and it was horrible," I said, trembling. Going back to that night in the woods wasn't easy for me. I had nightmares thinking about Johnny tied to that tree and then seeing him lying up in that hospital bed badly bruised. "I was the one who found Johnny in those woods. And it was horrible. My God, Reggie, what would make you do something like that to him? You need help."

"Why are you so worried about that faggot, anyway?" asked Reggie. He was now showing his true feelings. "He's been lying to you, too. He got what he deserved."

"How could you say that? No matter what you think of Johnny, he's still a human being," I said, shaking my head in disbelief. This was not the cousin who I had shared many family holidays, birthdays, and special moments with. Reggie used to be such a thoughtful, kind person. For my birthday last year, he sent me a dozen roses and a singing telegram that reminded me of what a special woman I was.

How could he have turned into this monster?

Reggie stood up and walked over to the corner of the room. He couldn't keep still for nothing in the world. "This isn't right. You defending him this way. I need you right now. Forget about that faggot."

"I'm sorry," I said, clutching my purse and wiping tears from my eyes. "But I can't help you with this. You need help, Reggie. This isn't the first time you've beat up on some gay person. That rumor about you in that gang fight years ago is probably true."

"So, that's it," he said. "Send me off to jail and throw away the key."

"I never said I didn't love you," I said. "But it's time you start taking responsibility for your actions. And don't worry, I'm not going to call your parents or tell Mom or Dad anything. I'll let you be the one to break the news, but you need to call them."

"Gee, thanks," he said sarcastically with a fake grin on his face, "for being so noble."

"I'll keep you in my prayers," I said on the way out the door.

"Just go then!" I heard him screaming as I rushed down the hallway. "I don't need you! I don't need anybody!"

"Ms. Edith"—I pressed the speaker button on the phone as I sat behind my desk—"hold all my calls this afternoon. And if Mr. Santiago shows up to work, please alert me as soon as possible no matter where I am in the building."

"Okay, ma'am," said Ms. Edith.

I immediately popped a pill in my mouth and washed it down with a glass of water. Dr. Abney had prescribed medication to calm my nerves. I was so frantic about everything lately. And seeing Reggie in handcuffs almost sent me over the edge. All of the drama was beginning to take its toll on me. However, Reggie was the least of my worries.

James had learned about that one stupid night with Johnny that I wished to forget. Apparently, Johnny couldn't stand lying to James. What a crock of shit. His entire life was a lie, but now he wanted to be Mr. Honest.

Of course, I was upset with him for playing the nice guy. I had hoped to take our secret to the grave. Hell, I didn't want anybody to know that I had slept with him. I wasn't proud of myself, of that moment. Now I had to live with James knowing the truth.

Moreover, I had this vision of James walking in my office door—with that Flo woman who almost stabbed Mr. Toole—and attacking me. In my opinion, James was still a violent man capable of anything. And after seeing his mother, I knew where that violence in him originated. The apple doesn't fall too far from the tree.

The phone rang.

"Yes, Ms. Edith." I pressed my head back against the chair. My skull was pounding. I felt sick to my stomach. "I thought I said hold my calls. What is it?"

"It's Lester, ma'am," she said. "He wanted to see you for a minute."

"Send him in," I said, sitting upright in the chair with a smile on my face. No matter what I was going through in my personal life, I tried to never show it to those kids. They needed my full attention.

"Good afternoon, ma'am," Lester said upon entering my office. He was so polite. I still couldn't believe that Mr. Toole was his father. "I wanted to give you this."

Lester handed me a card made out of construction paper. There were two simple but beautiful words written inside of it: "Thank you."

"This is so nice," I said, looking at the card as if it was the best gift in the world. It may have been construction paper, but it felt like gold. Lester lifted my spirits on an otherwise awful day. "Why are you thanking me though?"

"For being so nice about everything with my dad," said Lester. He pushed those glasses up on his nose. "I know he caused a lot of trouble."

"But nobody blames you," I said. "You're not responsible for your father's actions."

"Thanks for saying that," he said.

"How have you been?" I asked him. "Hope you've been okay."

"I'm good," he said with both hands in his pockets. I sensed he was nervous. Lester was such a shy kid. "I'm staying with my dad's sister for the time being. My dad said he has to get himself together."

"Well, you hang in there," I said as I walked with Lester to the door. "And if you ever need to talk about anything, you know where to find me."

Lester stopped in front of the door. He turned and stared at me.

"Is there something else on your mind, Lester?"

"I was wondering when Ms. J is coming back," he said with a sad look on his face. "We all miss him."

"Mr. Santiago is taking some personal time." I hated when the students called James Ms. J, so I made sure to correct Lester. It simply was inappropriate for a man to be called Ms. anything, especially in the workplace. "But I'm sure he'll be back to see you guys soon."

"Thanks again, Ms. Doggett," Lester said on his way out the door. He seemed satisfied with my answer.

As for me, I felt really sick. The pressure from everything that had been happening over the past couple of weeks had finally taken over my body.

I ran to the toilet in my office bathroom and vomited.

17

Johnny

"We're proud to accept you as a member of Gamma Phi Mu," said Dr. Nicholson. He was the president of Wheatley College and a member of the fraternity–a short man with slick hair and a quick grin. My family, including Uncle Leonard and Aunt Sabrina, were there to see him bestow this prestigious honor upon me. "You're given all the rights and privileges of a brother of the fraternity."

Everyone clapped and cheered. Man, Pops was damn near in tears. This was a moment he had waited to see since I was a kid. Going through the pain and suffering of the past week was worth it just to see that glow on his face–on both of my parents' faces.

"Thanks, Dr. Nicholson," I said, taking hold of the items inside his hands. Although I still had the casts on my arms, I was at least able to move around a bit. No doubt, I was getting better and better. Maybe it was the excitement of becoming a member of Gamma Phi, but I wasn't feeling any pain at all. "I will cherish these items forever."

Dr. Nicholson gave me a plaque, certificate, and T-shirt with the fraternity's logo and imprint. The plaque and certificate certified me as an official member. They were given to every new member. Pops, my uncle, and brothers all got a certificate and plaque hanging on their wall. There was a poem titled "Invictus" written on the front of the plaque. It was a poem that speaks to a man's struggle to make it in the world against forces beyond his control. They actually make every new member learn this poem and recite it at the initiation ceremony. That moment was stolen from me forever thanks to Reggie.

"Don't ever give up, young man," Dr. Nicholson said. "Like the poem says, 'You're the master of your destiny.' "

"For sure," I said. "That's for real."

Once again, I stared at the items and smiled. Although I was happy, man, I couldn't stop looking at the door and wishing James would walk in. It wasn't a complete celebration without him.

"Why don't you smile for the camera?" said Uncle Leonard. I was the son he never had. This moment had to be special for him, too.

"Wait, let me hold the plaque in front of him," said Carl. He walked over to the bed and raised the plaque and certificate on my behalf. I smiled wide and long for the camera.

"Oh, he looks so cute," Aunt Sabrina said. "Just like a Gamma man."

"Why don't all you Gamma Phi brothers take a picture together," Moms suggested.

Pops, Uncle Leonard, Dr. Nicholson, and Carl made a circle around my bed. They held both fists in the air—the official signature of Gamma Phi Mu. The raised fists were meant to show our unity and brotherhood.

"That's a great picture," Moms said, snapping the picture. "All these fine black men are too much for me."

"Just remember which one you belong to," Pops said, and kissed Moms on the cheek. It was always nice to see my parents flirting and loving one another.

"Before I go," said Dr. Nicholson, speaking to me and the entire family, "I would like to make it clear that our university has zero tolerance for hatred of any kind. What Reggie and the others did to you is unacceptable, and they will pay the price."

"We appreciate that, sir," said Pops. "This has been a difficult situation for everyone involved, and it means a lot to my family that you came down here personally."

"Oh, I wouldn't have wanted to be anywhere else," said Dr. Nicholson. He rubbed the top of my head. "I'm honored to have Johnny as a member of our fraternity. I had no problem getting this approved by the main office. Johnny has shown great strength and character—qualities of a true Gamma man. Those others could learn a lot from your son."

Hearing those words meant a lot. Ultimately, Reggie was arrested and most of the other members were expelled from school. Although Reggie was trying to protect members of the frat from going to jail, they ended up suffering in the end anyway. Dr. Nicholson had suspended the fraternity from the campus indefinitely, which couldn't have been easy for him. You know, being a member of the frat himself.

"Thanks for coming," Pops said, patting Dr. Nicholson on the back and walking him to the door. "God bless you and your family."

I stared at the fraternity T-shirt sitting next to me on my bed and started tearing up, man. It was hard to believe that I was really a member. You damn right I was still proud. Reggie and those other fools didn't represent the views of everybody in the frat. Gamma Phi Mu was made up of respectable men like my Pops and Uncle Leonard who paved the way for younger brothers like me and Carl. So there was no reason for me to hang my head. I took in the moment and owned it. Reggie wasn't going to steal my joy, man.

Uncle Leonard and Aunt Sabrina were getting ready to go. "Take it easy," Uncle Leonard said, and rubbed me on top of my head. "I love you and I'm proud of you."

"Thanks, Uncle, man," I smiled at him. "Thanks for coming."

"And I love you, too." Aunt Sabrina kissed me on the forehead. "Get some rest."

After a while, it was just me, Pops and Moms, and Carl left in the room. I kept staring at the door and looking at the items in my bed. Man, I felt like a kid on Christmas morning.

"Sweetheart, why don't you get some rest?" said Moms. "You've had such an active day. I know you must be tired."

"Has anyone seen James?" I asked, staring at the three of them.

"I told you earlier, son," said Pops. "He hasn't been around here today or yesterday. Maybe it's for the best."

"How could you say that, Pops?" I was quickly getting upset. "I love him."

I suddenly heard the door open and slam. Carl had abandoned ship. I guess he couldn't handle me expressing my true feelings for James out in the open. But I didn't care, man. This was my life—not theirs.

"Sweetheart, don't get yourself upset." Moms fluffed my pillow. "Your dad didn't mean anything by it. We love you."

"If you love me," I said, staring at the both of them, "then you should accept James in my life. Man, you should leave. Just wanna be alone."

"Son, don't be like that," said Pops. "We want you to be happy."

I gave him the silent treatment. Closed my eyes on both of them and pretended like I was sleeping. They got the message, man.

"We'll see you tomorrow, sweetheart." Moms kissed me on the forehead. "I love you."

When the door closed, I opened my eyes. Now that everyone was gone, I felt so empty and alone. Being in love will make you feel that way. No matter how much love you got in your life from family, if you're not with the one you love then you still can feel loveless. Man, I hated feeling this way, too. I had to go and open my stupid mouth and tell James about me and Sheila. Now I may have lost him forever. The walls felt like they were closing in on me.

"What's up, dude?" Steve asked as he walked into my room. I was hoping it was James, but it was his fake ass. I couldn't believe this nigga had the nerve to show up in my room after setting me up. You heard me right, man. That fake bastard set me up. Remember that confession inside his room? You know, the one where he claimed to be gay?

It was all an act, man. Reggie had put him up to it to find out if I was really gay. Members of the frat had become suspicious of my sexuality after seeing me on campus talking to Kevin. They used Steve to take me down.

"What the hell do you want?"

"I know I'm the last person you wanna see," he stated the obvious. "But I had to come."

"For what, man?" I said. "To see your handiwork? To make sure they did the job right?"

"I had no idea they would do this to you, dude." He stood in front of my bed with tears in his eyes. "I swear. I never knew it would get out of hand."

"You set me up," I said with bitterness. "There's nothing for us to say to each other. For all I know, you were one of the ones who attacked me at the cabin with Reggie."

"Don't be ridiculous, man," he said with a sincere look on his face. I couldn't tell if he was lying or not. Steve wasn't a trustworthy character in my book. You know, after setting me up inside his dorm room and having me believe he was gay. "I'm not that type of cat. You know that. I was angry when I found out what they did. I thought they wouldn't let you on the line—not try and kill you, dude."

"Whatever, nigga," I said. "Maybe you weren't there, but you're just as guilty."

Steve noticed the Gamma Phi T-shirt on the nightstand next to my bed. There was a longing in his eyes. Steve had always wanted to be a member of the frat. Now that Gamma Phi was suspended from the yard, his dream would never come true—at least not at Wheatley. He could still pledge graduate chapter, but it wouldn't be the same as pledging as an undergraduate. I guess there was some justice in the world, now that I had something that Steve desperately wanted.

"Is that what I think it is?" he asked.

"Yep," I said, smiling in his face. "I'm a member of the frat. Run back and tell your boys that."

"I'm happy for you, dude." He had that fake-ass grin on his face. "You deserve it after what they put you through."

"Steve, we'll never be friends," I said, cutting straight to the chase. He wiped that smile off his face. "I'm not interested in nothing you have to say. Get out. Go, man!"

I must have scared him, because Steve took out the door like demons were on his back. But he wasn't getting any sympathy from me. I had my own demons to fight. The only thing on my mind was James. How was I going to convince him to take me back?

I drifted in and out of sleep most of the night. Man, it was sad how I kept waking up and staring at the door. But it was pointless.

James wasn't coming. And I wasn't going to ever get any sleep.

SEVERAL
MONTHS
LATER

18

James

"Girl, this some good gumbo," said Mookie. He was sitting at the table and eating. You heard me right, honey. Mookie was eating my homemade gumbo. God is good. I saw him fight his way back from anorexia with therapy and faith, and I was overwhelmed with joy. "You put your foot in this shit."

"Don't thank me," I said, adding a little more seasoning to the pot. The gumbo was Flo's special recipe that she gave me before she went back home. Although I may not have been returning to New Orleans with her, I still wanted to feel at home, and gumbo was the closest thing to actually being there. "Thank Ms. Flo, honey. That girl taught me everything I know."

I sat at the table across from Mookie, watching him eat. It was a miracle how he bounced back from death's door. His natural color had returned; his skin was glowing. Don't get me wrong. Mookie was still skinny as hell, but you could see he was picking up weight again. He actually had meat on his bones.

"Damn, bitch. You just gone sit there and watch me eat?" asked Mookie. "Aren't you supposed to be getting this place together for Johnny?"

"What's up, peeps?" Johnny walked through the door right on cue. He was walking with crutches and being assisted by both his parents. He was another one of God's miracles.

Most of Johnny's injuries were a fading memory and he wasn't sporting any casts. Although he was on crutches, Johnny's arms and legs were healing at a rapid pace. His skin was so radiant that you couldn't even tell he suffered massive injuries to his face. My baby was back in full effect, and you know I was grinning like a cheetah, honey. "I know y'all ain't started the party without me."

It was Johnny's birthday and the gumbo was to celebrate him. We were at his apartment, and this was Johnny's first time home since the attack. For the past couple of months, he had been living with his parents. Mr. and Mrs. Lomack had insisted that he recover at their place.

"There's the birthday boy," I greeted him at the door with a big hug. It felt so good being in Johnny's arms, inside his apartment where we had shared so many memories. We had been through many tests the past year and somehow the two of us ended up together. Now that was the biggest surprise of all.

After he confessed about his little indiscretion with Sheila, I thought I would never be able to forgive Johnny. But I was wrong, honey. While he was recovering, Johnny made it his priority to win me back. This boy went to great lengths to prove his love for me, y'all. It was crazy. For two weeks straight, Johnny sent me roses. He had a singing telegram sent to my class. Thank God it was after school hours, as that would have been quite embarrassing in front of my students. And when none of that worked, he used his mama.

"Hey, James," Mrs. Lomack said, and kissed me on the cheek. "Good to see you, sweetheart." The two of us had actually gotten close during Johnny's recovery.

Mrs. Lomack was the one who convinced me to take Johnny back. You heard me, honey. She said her son was suffering and hurting. And I found out just how far a mother's love stretches. Her love for Johnny was wide and deep. I told Mrs. Lomack I would only come back to Johnny on one condition: she and Mr. Lomack had to support our relationship one hundred percent. There was no way I was going back to a life of having to fight to be with Johnny. It was no way to live. They had to be behind us or I was walking away for good.

"What's up, son?" Mr. Lomack patted me on my back. "Something sure smells good in here."

"I cooked gumbo," I said, sitting next to Johnny on the sofa and holding his hand. This was how it had been ever since we kissed and made up. We couldn't get enough of showing one another affection. "For the birthday boy, but y'all free to have some, too. As you can see, my friend Mookie done already started attacking the pot."

Mookie smiled and waved at everyone. He was on his third bowl. Ms. Girl was making up for lost time not eating.

Mr. Lomack squeezed my shoulders. He then rubbed his stomach. "I hope you made enough, 'cause a black man is hungry."

It seemed Mr. Lomack, with that wide grin on his face, was actually happy to see me. I can't tell you how good that felt, honey. My heart was about to explode from happiness. I don't mean to get all sentimental and dramatic either, but this was a huge moment in my life. Johnny's parents had finally accepted me—something I had always wanted from them but never had until now. All my dreams were coming true and there was no better feeling in the world, y'all.

"And how's the birthday boy feeling?" I stared Johnny in the face. Just couldn't keep my eyes off of him. "Want me to fix you some gumbo, too?"

"I'm good for now." He held my hand in his. While Mr. and Mrs. Lomack attacked the pot along with Mookie, we sat there on the sofa and had some us time together. You know, simply loving one another and appreciating the moment. He could have died. We could have broken up. Tomorrow was not guaranteed. If I learned anything this past year, that was the most important lesson. And I was not wasting a single minute letting Johnny know exactly how I felt toward him.

"I'm so happy," I said. "And it scares me."

"Why you scared?" he asked. "I'm here with you and I ain't going anywhere. There's nothing to be scared about."

"I know." I leaned against his shoulder. "But I keep waiting for the other shoe to fall."

"Man, let go of negative vibes," he said, caressing my chin. "We made it."

Out of the blue, there was a knock at the door. Johnny stared at me. I was staring at the door.

"Well, are you gone get that?" he asked playfully. "Or are you gone sit here and stare in my face the whole time?"

"Whatever," I said. "You ain't all that, nigga."

I swung the door open and was immediately greeted by a cold chill. "Sheila. What are you doing here? Is this about work?"

I had taken the last month off to help with Johnny's recovery efforts. Sheila actually had approved my leave of absence. In a way, I had found a new level of respect for her, too. We had made peace in our own way. All that stuff from the past I had already forgiven.

During her cousin's Reggie's trial, I could tell Sheila was hurting. They gave him two years for aggravated assault. I told Sheila at the trial that I wanted to start over and put our differences aside. She shook my hand and that was where we had left things. But her showing up at Johnny's front door unannounced was stirring things up inside of me. Shit, I was only human. I needed space and time to forget that she had slept with my man, honey.

"No, everything is fine at work," she said.

I noticed that girl had picked up some weight. What a difference two months could make, I thought to myself. Ms. Bitch wasn't looking all that good. Sheila was a pretty woman–I'll give her that much–but extra weight took away from her in some way. "I need to speak with Johnny for a minute."

I stared at her in disbelief. "About what?"

"What's up, Sheila?" Johnny joined me by the door on his crutches. "What's going on?"

"I'm sorry to interrupt your evening," she said. "But I was wondering if I could speak with you. Just for a minute."

I stared at Johnny. "I guess I'll give you'll a minute, then."

"Who's at the door?" Mrs. Lomack shouted from the table.

"Sheila," I said, staring at Mookie. By the look on my face, he knew I was pissed. "Said she had something to tell Johnny."

"Maybe she just wanted to wish him a happy birthday," Mr. Lomack suggested, trying to soften the tension inside the room. He knew this wasn't cool for Sheila to be showing up unannounced on today of all days.

"Is everything all right?" I asked Johnny as soon as he came back.

"Good as ever," he said with a straight face. I was waiting for that shoe to fall and land right on top of my damn head. "Everything is good."

"What did Sheila want, sweetheart?" asked Mrs. Lomack. I never took my eyes off Johnny. I thought his ass was acting really strange, or maybe I was just paranoid with all the shit that went down.

"Oh, she just wanted to wish me a happy birthday," he said, sitting down on the sofa.

"How did she did know it was your birthday?" I asked with an attitude.

"Tiffany told her," he said. "She talked to Carl and Tiffany."

"That was nice," Mr. Lomack said, sipping gumbo from his bowl. "She's a sweet girl."

I rolled my eyes at the comment and plopped down on the sofa. Johnny was now watching a football game on TV.

"What?" he asked. "Why you staring at me like that?"

"No reason," I said. "I can't look at you?"

"You can look at me whenever you like," said Johnny. He kissed me. He kissed me with his parents staring at us from the kitchen. That took my mind off Sheila and reminded me of what was really important. I had Johnny—not her. He was *all* mine.

"I think I'm ready for some gumbo," I said and stared at that door and then back at him—at the door and then back at him again.

"Give me a big bowl, too," he said. As I headed for the kitchen, Johnny shouted after me, "You know I can't get enough of you and your cooking!"

About the Author

Clarence Nero, an author, screenwriter, educator, grew up in New Orleans's Ninth Ward and earned a B.S. degree at Howard University. His first novel, *Cheekie: A Child Out of the Desire,* was critically acclaimed and was praised by the renowned poet Dr. Maya Angelou. His screenplay *Cheekie* was recently endorsed by Jonathan Demme, the Academy Award–winning director of *The Silence of the Lambs,* and was a finalist at the Sundance Lab. Nero has an MFA in creative writing from Louisiana State University. He teaches at Baton Rouge Community College.